HONOUR THY FATHER

HONOUR THY FATHER

LESLEY GLAISTER

BLOOMSBURY

First published in 1990 by Hamish Hamilton Ltd

This paperback edition published by Bloomsbury Publishing Plc 1999

Copyright © Leslie Glaister 1990

The moral right of the author has been asserted

Bloomsbury Publishing Plc, 38 Soho Square, London W1V 5DF

A CIP catalogue is available from the British Library

ISBN 0 7475 4205 8

10 9 8 7 6 5 4 3 2 1

Typeset by Hewer Text Ltd, Edinburgh
Printed in England by Clays Ltd, St Ives plc

For my mother
and my sister
and brothers

There goes Aggie again. Bang and crash and scrape all night. Where she gets the energy from I don't know. The wrong side of eighty, she is. And she wants this room, my room. But she has a room. We all have our own place. A room apiece. And this is *my* room. She's the eldest and she thinks it should belong to her because it's the biggest; because it was Mother and Father's room; because of the view from the window. I can't be doing with it myself, the flatness, not any more. Little skin of land stretched tight as a sheet and the sky billowing. All that weight of sky and no relief. Yet it's my room, fair and square.

It must be sixty years of banging and crashing and scraping just to prove a point. More than sixty years! Childish I call it – and the carpet's fair worn away. Bed under the skylight to catch the light? No, too draughty. In the low corner by the dressing-table with its pots and pots of old grease? No, too dark, too cramped. As if it matters! It's the attic room, where the twins used to sleep, with a sloping ceiling and narrow skylight of grubby grimy glass – for it's never cleaned. She doesn't care to crane her neck just to see the blessed sky, she says, and so the glass is green with growing things, tiny things that live in the wet. And yet she bangs and scrapes. *Evil old bitch*. Shout what you like, loud as you like. She'll not hear above the sound of her constant movement. *One of these days you'll go through the floor, Agatha!*

Even on Sundays. I said no relief. But if you strain your eyes, if the sky is perfectly clear, there is a kind of relief in the distant shine of the stone spire of the church in Witchsea beyond the dark bundles of trees and the odd roof. Just a faint glimmer, a tiny point on the horizon – but perhaps you can't see it at all. Perhaps it's one of those mirages, an image bounced off the tightness of the earth.

And then there's George. Poor baby George. Down there, below us all. Quite happy in a mindless, vegetable way. He is Agatha's. Never could do anything right, that one. But she doesn't help with him, hardly acknowledges his existence. She used to sing to him sometimes, those old songs, the ones Mother used to sing to us. But she doesn't do anything for him any more. No more use than ornament big sister Agatha since she's got old. I do not know what the twins think. The two of them – Ellen and Esther – are scarcely two at all but one and her reflection. And which is which? Mirror images they lean in when they walk, heads almost touching; one left-handed and one right. They walk in step; they talk often in unison. Ellenanesther.

They're young still – not seventy yet. They almost destroyed the house all those years ago, trying to pull down the wall between their rooms. They've got the smallest rooms because they match, long and narrow and dim with long windows facing out onto the fruit trees at the back. And they worked together, wordlessly, one each side of the wall, hacking and chipping until the house began to shake and creak. A crack slithered across my ceiling then – and it's there still. Inching across even now in a storm, or when Aggie has a really big shake-up. And they're left with a hole now. A two-brick-sized hole. They have their beds pushed against the wall, six inches apart, and when they lie down they can see each other's faces. Just watch each other until they fall asleep at the same instant and dream, I suppose, the same dream.

*   *   *

'Stay away from that dyke. Whatever you do. You hear me?' Every time he went away Father left us with this warning. And once he'd gone, like clockwork, we'd get up and do the chores. I did the laundry, the worst of the jobs – don't ask me how that decision was made – and the baking; Agatha did the outside work, and fed and milked the cow; the twins cleaned the house and helped us if we asked them to. With all of us working hard, four strong pairs of hands – even the twins were quite capable as long as they worked together – the chores were done by dinner time. The chickens and the cow tended; the garden seen to; the beds aired and the floors swept. And then – except for wash days – there was the long afternoon.

It was worst when it rained and blew. Then the sky would be full of whorls of rain and grit that flung and pelted against the walls that held us inside. Although I was quite content on those days because I was happy to be still. Sometimes I read an old newspaper of Father's, sometimes, when it wasn't too cold, I just sat, alone, in Father's room gazing out of the window. Already I loved that room, loved the sweeping endless view and knew that here I'd be the first to see him coming back. A little dot at first, steadily growing into a long shape; a pony and trap; and then into Father. And then, once he'd become Father again, he'd arrive home. And whether it was joy I felt, or whether it was fear, I was not certain. Anyone that went away from here, I used to believe when I was small, ceased gradually to be themselves, became nothing but a tiny dot. And then nothing at all. Unless they came back, as Father always did.

Ellenanesther used to sit by the hearth playing with their peg dolls, whispering in their private language, lives for their toys. Their voices were soft, scarcely audible, like rustling leaves. But little words would catch in the air sometimes: omotheromothero; thebloodandthemudandtheholygoat; wetollthemdead. The hearth with its arch of brick pointing up the furred black chimney was the church and the lives of the peg dolls were played out before it – the pairings and multiplyings and deaths – and when their blunt legs snapped they were sent via the flames to Heaven. For Heaven was up that chimney.

Agatha was the only one who liked to work in the afternoons, to work in the barn, forking the hay; splashing the brick floor clean; or outside in the garden hoeing between the rows of lettuces and beans, sending the weeds flying in muddy arcs. And once she'd tired herself out she'd go to Barley the brown cow and talk out her complaints about her lot – for Aggie was always complaining, always sighing – talk out her dreams. The animal would gaze calmly at her, past her, with wet brown pansy eyes, listening and blinking wisely her spiky lashes. And Aggie would doze sometimes, her ear against the warm tunnel of Barley's back, hearing the comforting gurgling and churning – but these times were rare, for Aggie was really a doer, with no time for idling – or idlers.

*   *   *

Sometimes, on hot days, when scarcely a breeze blew across the flatness, we'd walk along the narrow dusty paths, gathering blackberries or sloes or mushrooms or sometimes just a bunch of wild bright flowers. We always walked in a little procession. Aggie first, the eldest: she was nearly six foot tall, gawky in her pinafore and endless length of black stockinged legs; me, Milly, behind, plumper and shorter and never as beautiful, with my tow-coloured hair in a long plait down my back; and Ellenanesther at the back, leaning in, heads almost touching, like reflections. Thus we would walk, and sometimes – solemn and silent but for the rustling of Ellenanesther – we would turn towards the dyke.

We'd walk along the road beside the bank that was one side of the dyke. High above it towered, and behind it a wall of water, way above our heads. 'If ever the bank gave way,' Aggie always used to say, looking back over her shoulder at us dramatically, 'a twelve-foot wave would sweep the countryside, destroying everything. *Us first!*' And we'd all shudder in delicious terror, imagining such irresistible destruction.

And then we'd climb up from the road, up the steep side, and stand in a row along the top and watch the water. The sides were steep, dry and flakey at the top, a glistening chocolatey mud just above the water. Not much grew in this part of the dyke, save the occasional staunch bullrush, for the water flowed so swiftly. It was not clogged with life like the slower ditches and dykes, not like a friendly reedy willowy river bank. This water meant business. It was brown and opaque and the surface of it screwed up with the concentration of the rush it was in. It flowed away and away and away.

It had taken Mother away.

Father told me about the dykes once, when I was very little. He said that once this land was under water. He said the Romans dug ditches to drain the land for farming. And he said that later there were riots when it was done again, because people used to like the wet. They used to fish and catch the water fowl. They used to walk on stilts! But it was all drained. It must have been odd having the whole of your world changed like that. Having all the wet sorted from the dry. Over the years the land has blown away and sunk leaving these towering walls of water, of laboriously patched mud. They angle round the corners of ancient fields, some monstrous, some little more than ditches. We called this one Mother's Dyke because it was the one that had taken our mother.

From the way Father talked, it was almost as if he was afraid of the water. No, not afraid quite, more as if he didn't approve of it. He admired the people who drained the land, controlled the flow of the water. He sometimes travelled to Holland on business, and he said the land there was just the same, flat and tame, managed by man. He said it was a Dutch engineer who had drained the land, in likeness of his own country, in the seventeenth century. Yes, Father approved of the straight lines, the corners, the distinction between the wet and the dry.

Sometimes, disobediently, we would visit Mother's Dyke. We would hold vigil, clamber up the bank to see the water. Sometimes one of us would think that she saw something beneath the surface, nudging up through the wrinkles. Aggie and I knew that by now she would be nothing but a skeleton, so that it would be a skull that would appear, the water rinsing through the empty eye sockets, maybe an eel threaded round, maybe green weed flowing out like hair. But Ellenanesther who were only babies when Mother died saw something like a sepia photograph, a calm sad-eyed dignified face, a sweet smile, a white hat; they strained to focus on it among the brown ripples but could never quite get it clear. Lucky they had each other, these two, for they filled the space a mother would have taken, and Mother – the photograph on the mantelpiece; the unfocused flowing face in the dyke – was just an idea.

The longer she wasn't there, the more of a mystery Mother became. She had been a lady, that much was clear. She had talked like a lady and she had many manners. Ways. Ways that weren't common round here – at least our nearest neighbours, the Howgegos, didn't possess them. Father insisted on manners though, and so she kept them up. But that wasn't all there was to Mother. There was something bad and glamorous too, something that didn't fit with her lady voice. Something that Father didn't like to be reminded of, and that was the music and the songs. She had a piano, terribly out of tune, and rarely played, but still, a piano which gave the room an air. And she knew songs, really funny songs that would have us laughing and dancing on dark winter afternoons when Father wasn't here. The thing that was not quite respectable about Mother was that her father had been a music-hall artiste, a *real* artiste although her mother had been a lady. 'She married him for love,' Mother explained once, sighing, 'but it didn't work. There was something in her, after all, that didn't approve.' And she had been confused. Her father's world was exciting but wicked; her mother's, dull but good. This was what we knew about the woman who had been our mother. Also that we had loved her. Also that she had gone.

*   *   *

6

Big sister Agatha. Scraggy Aggie. Agatha, bitch name, witch name. Pain. Standing in the kitchen, so proud, as if she knows it all. Remembers it all.

'Remember the time,' she says, 'when our second cousin and his friend came to call? Home on leave. Heroes. And they spent two weeks cycling, and they came to call on us. Remember that time?'

I shrug. But there's no stopping her. And she stands still when she talks, at least, a far-off look in her eyes, making up memories while I get on with making tea.

'And I was wearing my pink dress with the blue sprig – my prettiest – and a wide hat with a pink rose on the brim, just here . . .' she looks at her ravaged reflection in the glass, 'and I looked a proper picture. Roses in my cheeks, roses on my hat of palest pink. I was tall and straight. *Slender*. And they came to call on me, us . . .'

'Oh no,' I say, for we must get it right, 'I remember that time too. I remember a stroll in the evening with the friend. It was evening, getting dark, and there were bats, and one nearly tangled in my hair, and I jumped and he steadied me with his arm. With his strong arm, soldier's arm. Roger, I think was his name.'

'Oh no dear, you've got it wrong. His name was Roderick, and it was *me* that he walked with. Impeccable manners too, and *my* arm that he steadied. He held my arm just above the elbow here, like this,' and she demonstrates, a proud little smile on her face, 'and he said how lightly I walked, how very . . . gracefully . . . I was tall and straight then, remember, slender.'

'And you muddied your dress . . .'

'I did no such thing. We walked together and the sun was setting and the sky was aflame and he said he'd come back . . .'

'But he never did. Did he? Did he?' I say, smashing eggs into a bowl. 'And he walked with me too.' Because he did. I remember. She will poach my memories. I have the room that she wants. She's never forgiven me for taking that room, the biggest and the brightest and the best room and now she tries to take my memories instead. But they are *my* memories, it was my arm he steadied – not that I care, it was Isaac I always cared about – and as he grasped me the back of his hand brushed the side of my breast. I can feel it still. The back of his soldier's hand against my breast, just at the side. A soldier's hand, a hand that had held a gun, killed perhaps, the enemy, brushing against *my* breast.

'I suppose you want some of this?' I say, beating and beating the eggs, smashing the yolks to slivers, the whites to foam.

'Since you're doing it,' she says, as if she couldn't care less. 'What was his surname then? Eh? If you know it all, go on, what was it?'

'Get me some chives,' I say. 'Take the scissors and snip me some chives. You know and I know that we never knew it.' I've got her there because it's true, we never did. She goes off, bent grey witch, into the garden, spiked scissors in her bony hand.

And it was my knee he touched when we sat on a cushion of clover. Inside my skirt. It was my knee, never Agatha's.

She comes back with a handful of hollow green spines tangled with grass. 'Chop them then,' I say, cross, for she is a useless article in the kitchen, my sister Agatha.

* * *

It was a hot dry day and the muddy side of the dyke was cracked and pale where the water level had fallen. Aggie squatted, her hands clasped round her knees. She kept sighing. She was pale.

'What's up with you today?' I asked.

Ellenanesther sat down too, dangling their feet over the side, little black boots banging against the side, sending dried flakes into the water.

'Something is wrong. I must have done something wrong.'

'What do you mean?'

'Look.' Agatha slid her hand inside her skirt between her legs, and when she brought it out her fingers were red and slick with blood. 'And there's pain here,' she said, pressing her hand on her belly.

'Are you cut?' I asked, staring fascinated at Agatha's scarlet fingers. Ellenanesther began to cry. Agatha wiped her fingers on the grass. 'No. I don't think so. It's from my . . . a little yesterday, but more today.'

'Have you told Father?'

Agatha looked at me as if I was stupid. She snorted and stood up. She looked into the water for a moment. 'Mother isn't there,' she said brusquely to Ellenanesther. 'Dry your eyes.'

*   *   *

And there's tea to get for George. My turn to feed him. Turns! That's a joke! Monday: my turn; Tuesday: my turn; Wednesday: my turn. Every blessed day my turn. Except Sunday. Aggie's supposed to feed him on Sundays, but I don't know. Perhaps he doesn't get fed at all. I really don't know. He never says. She prefers animals to people – that's what she says. That's what she used to say. You'd think she'd have a bit more time for George in that case.

We eat our omelette with the last of the bread and a cup of tea. There is no gin, which always makes me tetchy. Aggie chews, noisy as ever, with a far-away look in her eyes.

'Brown!' she says, suddenly, triumphantly. 'We did know his surname, and it was Brown!'

'Not Brown,' I say, scornful. 'Brown was never his name, that was . . .' but I can't remember. I must think, must say something or she'll think she's one up. And then it comes back, 'Brown was Father's partner! Pharoah and Brown or Brown and Pharoah, that's it!'

Agatha crashes down her fork. 'Not enough salt,' she says. 'Always the same. Bland.'

'Nothing to stop you doing it for once, the tea,' I say. 'Speaking of which, are you going to see to George?'

'George?' she says. 'Oh *George* . . . Well I must get on, dear. I've a lot to see to this evening; the cow, the chickens . . . the playroom.' She is quite mad. The cow is only bones in the barn. Aggie let her die. And I can't remember what happened to the

9

hens. And notice how she never calls it 'my' room, always the playroom, as if it belongs to all of us, as if she hadn't got a room of her own, as if she's deprived. 'I can't seem to get settled up there,' she says, 'I'm going to move the bed . . . when I've finished outside,' and she goes off, martyred, to the barn.

Well somebody had to have Father's room. We had the house to ourselves after Father, and we had to organize it somehow. The house is a square house, an old house now. There are two big rooms downstairs: the sitting-room and the kitchen. There is a pump in the kitchen, and the stairs rise up from there. On one side of the landing, facing the back, there are the two narrow bedrooms that Aggie and I used to sleep in as children and where Ellenanesther sleep now. At the front is my room, the biggest and brightest, the best room. And then the attic is Agatha's.

But I cannot put it off any longer. I take a deep breath before going down to George's room.

* * *

For a long time after Mother died we continued to go to church. Witchsea was nearly five miles away, too far to walk every week – Father insisted that we walked. Aggie thought it was humiliating to arrive on foot, just as if we were poor, but Father wanted to rest Pepper and anyway, he said, the exercise would do us good. About once a month we went and the evening before was spent in preparation. We used to bathe by the fire, Aggie and Ellenanesther and I, while Father kept out of the way, and then we'd twist each other's wet hair in rags. We'd toss and turn all night trying to get our tight knotted heads comfortable, praying for a fine day, praying that something exciting would happen.

Early on Sunday we'd be up, Aggie and I vying for the mirror to see how our ringlets had turned out. Ellenanesther didn't care, and anyway, they had only to gaze at each other. Then there were the chores to do and lunch to prepare and leave cooking slowly in the range. Father might have been very strict and very moral, but he didn't hold with all that superstitious day-of-rest nonsense. He would wear his best suit, and we wore clean white muslin dresses and petticoats and white bonnets and gloves. It felt special, the whole family out together like that. Special but sad too, for there was a very obvious hole next to Father, a hole that I could never ignore. I used to walk behind it, concentrating on that space, conjuring a vision of Mother, the wideness of her skirt, the neatness of the back of her head, until I could almost hear the swish of her skirt on the road.

We walked the five miles on the road which ran indirectly – following the seams of clay that threaded the low earth – to the village to keep our newly polished boots clean; but on the way home, if the weather was dry enough, we sometimes cut across the fields. When we were near enough to the village to see the spire our excitement would grow and our pace quicken. Any belief in God had been washed away with Mother – but Aggie and I longed for the congregation, for new faces, for other voices. There were plenty of young men there too, to stare at. Church-goers, a cut above the Howgegos, who were out-and-out heathens.

We were proud of Father too while others could see us, so smart in his Sunday suit, smart and sad and dignified. He was a businessman, important, dealing in crockery. He employed peo-ple; and in an area where work was scarce was a respected figure. We knew we made a handsome group, our father and his four girls, and would revel in the eyes of the congregation, and though as eager as anyone to have a good look round would appear aloof. At least Aggie would; tall and elegant, she had a way of tilting her chin that seemed to add to her inches. She knew the congregation must be full of young men who would set their caps at her when the time was right. Her future husband might even be there now, his eyes fixed longingly upon her.

*   *   *

Mush he eats. White mush. I don't think it matters. I don't think he tastes it. I don't think there are any teeth left in his mouth. The rages have stopped anyway, mostly. White blubber, pale body, pale eyes blinking at the light I need to see. I think he prefers the

11

dark. Hardly a flicker on his face. Impassive now. Pale fat lips open. Spoon it in, the white mush. Hold breath against the stench. Sometimes he swallows straight away. At other times gobs of it come back, white on his chin, and I scrape them off and push them back in. Think about something else.

Think about – try not to think about – Father. All right, but try to go back to before. Remember him as he was, before. Smart. A smart man, a little stout, very fussy about his appearance. 'Distinguished' sounds like the right word, with thin brown moustaches, brown hair. He was, above all, respectable. He liked to be seen to do, liked us to do, the right thing. Did I love him? Impossible to remember. I hardly remember him before Mother died. Big hands he had, long fingers. Sometimes he'd pick us up, one of us, Aggie or me, and swing us round in terrifying swooping circles, feet flying out, till when he set us down we staggered, bumped into the furniture and made him smile.

He was a good provider, that's what Mother said about him. Certainly we always had money and after he died some complicated trust has kept us just above the bread line, kept the wolf from the door. Some complicated trust! But love? I don't know. You never did know where you were with him. He was mild mostly and distant, but sometimes he would change suddenly, grow sharp teeth and pounce. Sometimes Mother was wary of him. Her movements would shrink when he came in, caged, cagey. She would stop singing. She knew so many songs, funny songs, and she sang well and danced and made us laugh and laugh. There was this song about Fashionable Fred, her joking name for Father – when he wasn't there. It went something like . . . *Of me you may have read, I'm Fashionable Fred, And no matter where I chance to show my face . . . I'm looked on as the cheese, and all the girls I please, I'm a model of elegance and grace* . . . I don't remember the tune, but Aggie does. That's one thing she does remember properly, tunes. Like Mother in that way, Aggie, musical. Mother could have been an actress! But I never saw her sing and joke and dance around the kitchen when

Father was about. She was quiet and demure then. Perhaps she *was* an actress.

She was, well, sugar and spice and all things nice like in the nursery rhyme, like little girls are supposed to be made of and aren't. She was warm and soft. I've never felt anything like that since, like the feeling when she picked me up and cuddled and stroked and soothed away the hurt. Maybe she was angry sometimes and sad. I try not to remember, and anyway, memory plays us tricks.

Ellenanesther don't remember at all. They were only babies when she died, just one year old, just staggering. They would have died too if it hadn't been for Aggie and me. Only little girls ourselves we were but we'd already half taken over from Mother before she left us. We copied her and chopped up food for Ellenanesther and kept them clean. We didn't have much of a heart for playing with them though, and they soon turned in upon themselves, leaning in, muttering in a language that only they could understand. Pretty they were, prettier than Aggie, for her good looks were more serious; and prettier, certainly, than myself.

We seemed to manage all right, and once Father had decided that we could, he shut himself out. There was some talk of getting a woman in from the village to keep an eye on us, but it never came to anything. He did not like us to see anyone. As time went by he became more and more insistent that we should not, should never see anyone from the outside. He would always ask. His first question would always be, 'Who have you seen? Has anyone been here?' and we always answered 'No'. And usually that was true. Apart from this obsession with keeping us apart from the world he was very little involved with us. His life was his work and whatever else he spent his time doing when he was away from home. In the winter he'd stay away for days. We never knew quite when he'd be back. He'd eat his breakfast silently before he left, and bid us be careful as he went, rubbing our heads, one, two three, four, and mind the dyke and he'd be off.

We'd hear Pepper's hooves and the squeak of the wheels and he'd be gone. Sometimes he stayed away a week or two, in town, sometimes he went further, abroad even, on business, and left us for weeks. I minded at first, missed him, though really we managed just as well without him. Later we were grateful when he stayed away.

I used to spend hours watching for his return, never believing until I saw him that he would, for after all Mother never did.

When he did come home it made a change. Aggie would go out and feed and groom Pepper while I made more of an effort with tea than usual. He would bring back groceries. We enjoyed unpacking them; tight brown bags of flour and sugar, and tea to decant into the caddy; bacon and currants and cheese; and sometimes for a treat, humbugs or toffee or, best of all, tiger nuts for us to chew. Twice a year there were clothes too, dresses made in the town. We chose the stuff from little square sample books which he borrowed and brought home for us to see. How I longed to go into town, or at least to the village, myself, on a weekday when there was a shop or two open, to go and buy something myself. But Father had forbidden it.

For a long time I tried to talk to him, ask him about his business, his friends in town. But he didn't take me seriously, would make some flippant remark, maybe pat me on the head. I wanted to know about his work. I never understood quite what he did, but he would sometimes bring home the crockery and the tiles that he dealt in. The kitchen walls are lined with Dutch tiles that Father said were very old, even then. They are blue and white with pictures of shepherds and sheep and children playing on them. Mother liked them. Clean and bright she said they were, nice in a kitchen – I think they were the only thing she liked about the house. Now, those that are left on the walls are grimy and cracked, and the stuff between them has rotted away into black softness. The crockery Father brought home was mostly blue and white too. Mother arranged the plates on the dresser in the kitchen: a big oval plate for meat with a ship sailing across it surrounded by curls of waves and clouds, and smaller plates with different pictures on them. On ordinary days we used the blue-and-white crockery, but Mother had another tea-service. It had been her grandmother's and so it was very old and precious. It was fragile, creamy, with tiny yellow roses, and the edges of the plates and saucers, the rims of the cups and the milk-jug were traced with gold. It was so old that the surface was covered with a fine crazing of cracks, like hairs. Flimsy, Father thought it, but Mother cherished it. Just sometimes she'd unpack it from its wrappings of paper and we'd drink tea from the frail cups. The tea used to taste extra delicious to me, as if some of the gold from the rim had come off on my lips. Mother crooked her finger like a lady when she drank tea from one of her grandmother's cups. After she left us, Aggie and I still got the tea-set out sometimes, just to wash and dry the cups, just for the elegant feel of it. Sometimes when Father came home I'd set it out to try and remind him, make him think of Mother – but if he noticed, he never said. I wanted him to talk to me, to talk about Mother, but he hardly mentioned her. Only sometimes I would see him gazing at her photograph, a strange expression on his face.

There was only one photograph. It's on the mantel now, faded, until it's almost gone, a faint face floating up through a pale sepia sheen.

*   *   *

On a hot windy day about a month later Agatha was once again pale and withdrawn. After lunch she sat still in a chair by the hearth vacantly watching Ellenanesther's game. I was about to go upstairs, with a handful of currants and a book, but I paused in the doorway, studying her.

'What's up?' I asked.

'Same as before . . . *you know*,' said Agatha. 'It makes me feel, I don't know, not like working.'

I felt a cold flutter of fear then. It wasn't like Aggie to be so still. 'We must do something!' I said, and then suddenly I realized what we could do. 'I know! Why don't we go and see Mrs Howgego! Could you talk to her?'

Agatha thought for a moment. 'Yes, I suppose so,' she said. 'Yes, I think perhaps I could talk to her.' And so that was a day of change. Excited, we got ready and we set out, and our walk was more purposeful than usual. It was for Aggie that we were going, but my mind was full of Isaac. Isaac my friend. Please please please, I muttered in time with my footsteps, please let him be there.

Although it was so hot, a strong wind buffeted and blew the earth around, and whipped the loose strands of our hair sharply into our faces as we walked the two miles to the Howgegos' red brick house. It was tiny in the distance, a ship moored in the flatness.

'Mrs Howgego was a good friend to Mother, wasn't she?' I said, hurrying to catch Agatha up.

'Yes she was.'

'She is a saint. Mother said that about her. That she is a saint.'

'That's not what Father said.'

'He doesn't know anything. What is it he hasn't got? In that rhyme? Gentility?'

'Don't be stupid, Milly,' said Agatha looking down her nose at me.

'Well that's what Mother said, and Mother wasn't stupid.'

'She didn't say that actually. But Father will be angry if he finds out we've been to see Mrs Howgego. We'll have to lie. Mother said that was all right sometimes. You don't say anything to Father. Understand?' Aggie called back to the twins. There was little fear of this, for the twins hardly said a word to Father, but it made their blue eyes grow round with importance.

'Yes Agatha,' they said.

'I think he's mad, Father,' I said. 'Don't you Aggie? One day we'll have to get used to seeing people. One day we'll go. We can't stay locked in that house for ever.'

'We're not locked in,' pointed out Agatha.

'Well that's what it feels like. I just want to be normal. I just
want to . . . just to . . .' I groped for what it was I wanted. 'Just to
be one of the world.'

'Well anyway,' said Aggie, 'we're out now.'

'Do you remember when we were always seeing Mrs Howgego
and the boys. Mother would make tea for them and lemonade for
us. We had fun.'

'There was that picnic.'

'By the dyke. And Isaac and I climbed a tree and – Oh I wish
she hadn't gone and left us,' I said, suddenly angry. 'It's not fair!'

'It's no use going on like that,' said Agatha. 'What's done is
done.'

We could hear the shouts of the young Howgego boys playing
with a rope tied to a tree long before we got there. Then the boys
caught sight of us and shouted, 'Mam! We got some company!'

Mrs Howgego came hurrying out. 'Bless me, we have and all!'
She came forward to meet us, smoothing down her wispy hair.
'Well, I never expected to see you here again! And will you look
at them twins! Talk about two peas in a pod! and Agatha, how
you've grown. Bless me if you aren't the dead spit of your poor
mother!'

I shot a jealous look at Aggie. It was true, of course, and truer
still the more she grew up. Aggie was tall and dark and ivory
skinned. She was almost a beauty. She just stopped short of it –
her big sharp nose saw to that. Still, she looked like Mother, like
the photograph of Mother. And the twins and I were all dumpier
and mousier – though we had our father's bright blue eyes.
Aggie's were dark, startlingly dark and long lashed – just like
Mother's had been.

'Well then, you better come in now you're here,' said Mrs
Howgego, 'out of this blessed wind, and shake some of that dust
off you.'

The kitchen was cluttered and messy. Mrs Howgego cleared a
space on the table, and tipped cats from the chairs to make room
for us. 'I'll make us some tea,' she said, 'in honour of this

occasion,' and she laughed at our solemn faces, reminding me with a pang of my mother. She had teased us like that sometimes . . . curtseying, treating us like royalty. 'Yer 'ighnesses,' she would call us in her put-on cockney voice, Aggie and I, sitting at the table at home, and she would serve us soft-boiled eggs and dainty fingers of bread and butter.

'Well then,' Mrs Howgego said, 'that's obvious that there's something up . . . you've all got faces longer than fishing poles. Are you going to tell me what's the matter?'

Aggie flushed scarlet and hung her head. I could see that she was not going to speak.

'It's Agatha,' I said. 'She's not well. She's got something wrong, a pain . . . blood . . .'

'Is that all!' breathed Mrs Howgego. She moved towards Aggie, and stroked her hair. Aggie jumped. We were not used to touch. Mrs Howgego laughed. 'That's quite natural at your age, girl,' she said. 'I suppose you haven't told –?'

'We couldn't talk to *Father!*' I said. 'Not about anything under our skirts.'

'Milly!' said Agatha. 'What a thing to say!'

'Well it's true.'

'Quite right too,' said Mrs Howgego agreeably. 'But you have to have someone to tell. I reckon that father of yours needs seeing to, leaving four great girls all alone like that. That's not as if he doesn't know the ways of the world.' She shook her head and smiled at Aggie. 'Well I never did! You poor old girl! Fancy not knowing about the curse!' She patted Aggie's shoulder. 'You need a mother, the lot of you.' She looked at the twins, 'Haven't you got a word to say to your Auntie? I remember when you was born. Never expected the two of you we didn't. Never even thought of it. She weren't even that big, your poor mam. Could have knocked me down . . . There was one of you, already in your mam's arms, and then she starts pushing away again, a proper frightened look on her face. "Candida," she says to me, "Yes dear," I says. "I think there's another," she says and right enough there was the other one. Didn't know whether to laugh or cry. Tiny you were then, I've never seen tinier that's lived. Talk about peas in a pod . . .' Ellenanesther smiled their identical smiles first at Mrs Howgego and then turning in to each other.

'They don't say much,' explained Aggie, 'except to each other. They talk to each other all right.'

'But never to you?' Mrs Howgego looked more closely at them and they hung their heads. 'Are they all there then?' she asked.

'Yes!' I said. 'Of course they are!'

'It's just that they don't seem to need anybody else,' explained Aggie. 'But they do need each other. I don't know what they'd do if they were separated.'

'They even go to the privy together,' I added.

'Well I never did!' said Mrs Howgego shaking her head. 'They ought to get out there and play with my boys, that would soon sort them out. Would you like to go out and play?'

Ellenanesther hung their heads and flushed. 'I don't think so, thank you,' I said for them.

Mrs Howgego shrugged. 'Now, you,' she said looking at Agatha, 'can come upstairs with me and I'll find you some rags. You mustn't worry yourself. That's just the curse, your month-lies, and that shows you're a woman now. If that doesn't come one month that's when you should be worrying! That means a babe's on the way. Not that there's any prospect of that till you're married,' she added hastily. 'As long as you keep yourself nice.'

She led Aggie upstairs. I went and stood by the window and watched two of the boys chasing a hen round and round making it squawk and scatter feathers.

'What are you gawping at?' said a voice, suddenly, from behind me. I jumped and turned round to face a tall freckly boy with a thick thatch of hair falling in his eyes. Isaac.

'Nothing,' I retorted.

He grinned and whistled through his teeth. 'The curse,' he said, 'your sister . . .'

'You were listening!' I said, blushing on Agatha's behalf.

'There's not much I don't hear,' he boasted. He looked at the twins. 'Got a screw loose then, have they?'

'No they haven't!'

'All right,' he said, grinning. 'That don't make no difference to me.' He stood staring at me with his flat blue familiar eyes until I felt hot and embarrassed. 'Milly,' he said at last.

'Isaac,' I said.

'That's me.'

'You've grown,' I said, for my old playmate Isaac had been shorter and plumper, though no less grubby than this towering boy. 'We used to play together, ages ago . . .'

'Before your mam done herself in.'

I flinched at that. Already it was all coming back. The way he teased, the way he dared me. But I was not ready for his teasing. We had been quiet for too long, I had forgotten how to do it. 'Before Mother died,' I corrected stiffly.

'Mother! Why don't you say mam like anyone else?'

'Mind your own business! I thought your mo . . . mam told you to get out. I'll tell her you've been listening!'

Isaac flushed. 'You!' he said, 'you look as if you're going to blab.'

'Not until you do!' I said, straining against the lump in my throat. I had missed Isaac so much. I had not even known how much until now. And now we were fighting.

'That don't bother me if you do tell my mam,' he said. 'She can't do nothing to me.' But he went towards the door.

'But she could tell Mr Howgego . . .' I said.

'He's away, and so are Abe and Ben, eel-catching up March way, so I'm the man around here for now.'

'Man!' I sneered. Isaac gave me a furious blue look and then turned and slammed out of the door. I stood smouldering, watching from the window as he stalked away. I turned and looked at Ellenanesther, who were oblivious to the argument and to Isaac, playing hand over hand, and muttering and giggling.

'Oh can't you stop it!' I shouted. 'Why can't you be like everyone else!' They stopped their game and looked at me with their blank shut-in eyes.

'Sorry Milly,' they said together, and sat in silence.

'Oh never mind,' I muttered. It didn't do to get angry with Ellenanesther. Whatever they did was innocent. Whatever.

Mrs Howgego gave us a loaf of warm bread to take home with us that first time, and I carried it, wrapped in a cloth to protect it from the hot dust that blew steadily across the land. We hurried. For what if Father had arrived home while we were out? When we'd gone a little way Isaac jumped up and greeted us as if he hadn't seen us before, let alone fallen out with me not half an hour before. Always I was astonished by the way his temper would fizzle and die almost as soon as it began. My own smouldered on, would smoulder on, for ever.

Isaac walked some of the way with us, beating at the long grasses at the edge of the road with a stick and sending out showers of grasshoppers and other buzzing creatures. He said little to me and nothing to Agatha, but dropped back and walked with the twins, stopping to point things out: 'That there's a cricket! See him . . . he's gone . . .' and 'That butterfly there he's a Red Admiral,' and 'Woolly bears look! Mind out for them, they make you itch!'

And all the time Agatha walked ahead, proud and queenly, her head held carefully upright like a new cap of knowledge which must not be spilt.

But I could not stay angry with Isaac in the way I could stay angry with others, in the way I stayed angry with Agatha. And although I was irritated with him that day, it was nice having him there. It lightened the atmosphere, for we were a solemn lot, hurrying, anxious. In Mrs Howgego's kitchen, with the boys larking about outside and the woman's cosy way of rattling on I'd felt it, how quiet we were. It made me remember, sharply, how it was when Mother was there, how Aggie and I used to play by the fire, or outside the back door, running to Mother with tell-

21

tales, and for hugs and kisses. How Mother had always made everything all right.

We never played so much once Mother had gone. Hardly ever laughed. There was work of course, and the babies to care for. They were nursed alongside our bewilderment and grief. Mother's going splintered us somehow, and Father couldn't hold us together. Oh we stayed together and the walls of the house contained us, but they did not hold us safe. We rattled inside, locked in our own heads – but for the twins who grew as one.

*   *   *

We're more together now than ever we were then. In the evening, like this evening, we'll spend time together. The hearth is empty of flames since the evenings have been warm and light. It's June. Must be around the longest day, and despite the rain that has been pouring down almost all day it is not chilly. There is the fresh earthy smell of summer rain drifting through the broken window; and wet pewtery light falls on the red brick of the arch, on the cobwebs in the corner.

I like cobwebs: tight stretched silk when they're new, shiny – works of art; and when they're old they drop soft and dusty and shrunken, so soft you can hardly feel them brushing you.

In the evenings we knit, Aggie and I, and sometimes, even, we play cards. These games are the first since our childhood. Rummy. It took a lot of time, a lot of argument before we remembered the rules. It takes concentration, patience – and Aggie so wants to win. It wouldn't bother me if it didn't bother her so much. I wouldn't care if *she* didn't. And so, because there must always be a winner and a loser, there are always fights. Not physical, *oh* no, but words, lashing words that whip us back, slash open the skin over our memories so they spill out confused and jumbled. We make of them what we can, what we will.

But tonight we knit, one each side of the empty hearth listening to the pouring of the rain, the occasional drop that finds its way down the chimney, and to the click of our needles and Agatha's sighs. Why she must always sigh I don't know. Ellenanesther are in the kitchen making their tea. They eat after us always, and always cold food, arranged like doll's food on their plates. They love to cut things up: a square of cheese apiece; half a tomato; a cucumber ring; bread and butter cut into tiny squares. And they eat the same things at the same time, chewing in unison. We leave them to it, clear our stuff out of the way – or I do more often than not – and leave them to it. Only, after they have finished I put away the knives. I like to put away, to count the knives, for they are dangerous things and must be treated with respect. I count them and I shine the blades, and then I put them in the dresser drawer.

Aggie's cats are piled in front of the hearth, most of them, or draped on the backs of chairs and on window-sills. It's a greyish tabby pile, like grubby washing, a purring, breathing heap. She knows the names – or claims she does. I don't even know how many there are now. When Mark, the boy, comes in his van with our groceries on, I think, alternate Friday afternoons, there is more cat food than anything else. There are biscuits, of course. Lots of them, gingernuts and bourbons and pink wafers and fig rolls and chocolate digestives and custard creams; and there's tea and condensed milk (since the milkman won't come here, and anyway we love the sweetness) and bread and cheese and eggs and olives, oh I love olives! and other bits and pieces. I like a nice slice of ham on Sunday, with a spot or two of mustard. And always a bottle of gin.

'*What* is it that you're knitting?' says Agatha suddenly, spitefully.

'It doesn't signify,' I reply. I will not rise to her bait tonight.

'You've been at it long enough. How many years is it? Will it be ready for Christmas?' She cackles at her idea of a joke, but I do not laugh, nor even smile. The important thing is that I'm knitting. The important thing is the rhythm of it, the clickety clickaclicka of the needles knocking their tiny heads together over and over and over. 'Socks for the boys in the trenches was it?

Or something nice for the painters? A matinee jacket for George? A cosy shroud?' She cackles again. Witch. I cannot resist her teasing. I knit tighter, pulling the old wool tauter and tauter until it snaps. Another knot.

Agatha begins to sing. Her voice is not what it was. I cannot believe the words she sings:

'You should see the weeping women with their
    faces white as cheese;
they seem to moan and shake their fists like me;
There's a sympathetic look upon every cabbage leaf;
and a broken ladder hanging from a tree.'

'That's never right, Agatha!' I say.

'What is it then?' she says. 'Go on, if you know so much you sing it.' She smirks and I simply cannot be bothered to answer. I can hardly see to knot my dark wool, disappearing in the gloom.

Agatha knits with bright pink nylon she orders from a catalogue. She likes catalogues. Anything she can get like that, free. She strains her eyes for hours at a time, sighing. If only we could afford new clothes – but there is no money to spare. It is years since we had new clothes. Aggie wore out all Mother's, and then we used to send off for things, dresses and cardigans and shoes, but there has not been the money for a long time. I still wear the last dress I bought. It is horrible, a horrible shiny indestructible material. No, it is not indestructible, it will melt. I brushed the sleeve over a candle one morning and melted a black hole which is there still, irritating, black and stiffened like a scar.

The postman will not come out here. It is not the distance, the post office explained, it is the fact that there is no road here, just a track that comes close. Mark manages though in his van. Our hero! And he brings the post too, and he takes Agatha's letters. She is the only one who writes letters, and gets letters. She likes to make a performance of opening the envelopes, so important. She knits doilies for the sideboard. It is thick with them. She knits antimacassars for the antimacassars; egg-cosies and tea-cosies and frilly jam-pot covers that soon grow thick and sticky with jam and mould; she knits blankets for the cats, to heap in the corners, to weave with their hairs. She knits them all in bright cheap indestructible nylon. But they have no meaning.

*   *   *

Mrs Howgego began to call. She'd come toiling along the path, and I'd usually spot her first from my perch on Father's window sill, a large billowy figure with two or three little clouds of dust – her boys – racing ahead of her. She always carried a big wicker basket, and in the basket, always there was something for us: an apple dumpling, or some raspberries, or a pot of damson cheese.

She'd come straight into the kitchen, no knocking, no standing on ceremony, for she saw us as children, children playing house, and this incensed her. Four great girls and no mother! she'd mutter, rustling in, muscling in, her arms in the sink, her head in the cupboard almost before she'd said how do. In fact our house, then, was tidier than hers but she never saw this, saw only that the apples were falling and past their best for storing, or that Agatha had let the lettuce bolt.

All the same, we always enjoyed her visits, listened without complaint to her fussing, brewed her pots of tea. The twins would stand and look round-eyed at her while she clucked at them twopeasinapod and IswearIneverdid. They smiled, pleased to have their identical identity so confirmed.

Agatha played up to her of course. After all, she was the oldest and a woman now. Mrs Howgego herself had said so. This was what the blood and the pain meant, a new importance. She used to stare at herself in the old mirror. I saw her peering, turning her head this way and that. From the front she was beautiful, looking in the mirror she could see beauty and she smiled Mother's smile and was satisfied, but if she turned her head she could see that her nose was wrong. Too long, too sharp. Ugly? Beautiful? If only someone would say. She would turn away from the mirror, impatient.

Aggie played the hostess to Mrs Howgego with some grace, arranging the tea things prettily, offering a seat, finding scraps to say – 'How are you Mrs Howgego? and the boys? Warm enough for you Mrs Howgego? Looks like rain.' – and not forgetting to offer cake and glasses of milk to the boys. Between them there was common ground, and I was excluded, Agatha made that quite clear, for they were both women and I was still a little girl. Now and again the visitor would lean forward confidentially, sometimes even grasping Agatha's hand, 'Everything shipshape?' she'd ask, lowering her eyes towards Agatha's belly.

And Agatha would blush and nod, 'Quite in order, thank you,' flattered and ashamed.

And there was gossip too. When Father stopped coming home regularly he arranged for Sara Gotobed who ran the village shop to deliver our groceries – which were paid for direct from the bank. Mrs Gotobed was a stout whiskery woman whom Mrs Howgego could not abide. 'They're a bad batch them Gotobeds,' she'd say. 'Mind you don't go listening to any of her nonsense.'

We did listen, of course, but we did not believe, for she said bad things about Mrs Howgego. They said bad things about each other, but it was Mrs Howgego we believed. Mrs Gotobed attended all the births in the village and she was angry that Mother had not chosen her for her confinements. I suppose that was why she never liked us much, never had much time for us, except to pause now and then and say evil things about our friend.

'You want to watch that Candida Howgego,' she'd say, nodding in the direction of the Howgego house. 'There's never a month goes by without her trying to cheat me out of a farthing for this, or a halfpenny for that. And what her old man gets up to is nobody's business but I reckon half the babes born in the village have that mean old Howgego look to 'em.'

We smiled wisely, not sure what she meant and certainly not believing a word of it. We didn't like Sara Gotobed much, and Aggie and Ellenanesther kept out of the way when she called. I

26

used to talk to her a bit, but she didn't like me. I could see she didn't and so in the end I kept away too.

Mrs Howgego was pleased when I told her that we didn't like Sara. 'I should weigh out every last thing she brings you,' she advised. 'She sold me short on soap last month, and flour the month before – and then there were moths in it. And you should see the state of her house! That's a wonder she manages to hang on to that man of hers . . . that's only fear of her tongue that does it. She's got him wound round her pinky like a bit of string.'

Whenever I saw that Isaac was with his mother, I'd run to meet him, hot and breathless with excitement, and embarrassed by my own eagerness – for it was only with Isaac that I could be a proper child.

We'd greet each other awkwardly and Mrs Howgego would shake her head at the pair of us until we trailed off round the back to pelt apples and stones at a target he'd drawn on the barn wall; or balance in the low boughs of the fruit trees and talk.

'I'm getting away from here soon as I can,' he said once, his face screwed up with the sourness of the early apple he was eating.

'You'll get collywobbles,' I warned, having suffered similarly myself. 'Away where?'

'The army maybe,' he said, picking at a scab on his knee.

'The army!' I looked at him with admiration imagining a picture-book soldier, red frogged jacket, shiny buttons, a grey horse. 'Away from here, anyway,' he said.

'I might . . . miss you,' I said. I felt embarrassed to mention a feeling.

Isaac squinted at me and then looked away, flushing. 'Mam says that's all very well us being, friends now like, while you're still a girl. But she says you'll be a woman soon and then it wouldn't be . . . nice . . . being, you know, alone together.' He looked back at me and wrinkled his nose. 'Though you don't look much like a woman to me,' he added.

I looked down at my flat neat child's body. 'No,' I said. 'I don't do I? Aggie's one though, and she doesn't look it either.'

'Funny that,' he agreed.

'But I hope you won't stop being my friend, Isaac. I won't be able to help it, you know.'

'But you might not want to do things,' he said, 'when you are one. You might want to do other things instead.'

'What do you mean? Like what?'

'Oh I don't know. Woman's things. I don't reckon you'll still climb trees. You'll have to keep yourself nice.'

'Your mam says babies come if you don't keep yourself nice.' I pondered for a minute. Surely climbing a tree wouldn't make a baby come? I felt his eyes upon me and when I looked up he was looking at me strangely.

'Don't you know nothing?' he asked. 'How you get babes?'

Hot blood rushed to my cheeks and I jumped down from the tree so that he wouldn't see. 'Anyway, if you're joining the army you'll be gone by the time I'm a woman.'

'You don't, do you? Haven't you ever watched your Barley being served? Or the chucks with the old cockadoodledoo?'

A flutter of squawking feathers flashed through my mind; the triumphant bellow of the bull. I picked up a hard green apple and flung it at the barn, hitting the centre of the target with a dull thud. 'Don't believe you,' I said, although I did.

Those times were good. Those odd ordinary days when I was not odd, but ordinary. A little girl with a long plait. A little girl with a friend. Once we raced to Mother's Dyke for a dare, to see if they noticed we were gone. As we stood looking into the brownness of the water I talked about Mother, how perhaps she was in there still.

'I reckon she'll be out at sea by now,' he said. 'In Africa maybe. That's not the same water anyway, that's different water all the time.' We pondered this for some time. I had never thought before that the water that streamed past endlessly was different water, new water that poured forever away.

'Where does it all go?' I said.

'The sea,' he said.

'I've never seen the sea.'

'Nor've I. But I reckon I will,' he said proudly. 'When I go away from here.'

'You'd think the sea would fill up and flood over,' I said.

'Perhaps it will,' he replied.

'But where does all the new water come from?'

He looked frowningly along the flow of the dyke. He never liked to admit to not knowing anything. 'You're daft you are,' he said.

'I never am.'

He looked at me speculatively. 'You are an odd bod. Sort of different. That must be funny, having no mam.'

'It was at first,' I said, 'but not now, not any more. I can't imagine having one now. *That* would be odd. But nice.'

'She went mad my mam says.'

'She never did!'

He shrugged. Sometimes he was wise, Isaac. Sometimes he let things be. A pair of grebes bobbed past. 'Let's swim,' he said.

'No!' I jumped back. This was the water that had taken Mother.

'Come on, cowardy!' He pulled off his shirt and trousers. White he was and long. I giggled, surprised by his thing, a little pale sausage. But then he jumped and I was gripped with fear. I saw his buttocks flash, blue white, and then I couldn't look.

Mother was in there. And now he thrashed his eel-like body, his long toes, into the depths. He might tread on her face. I turned my back, trembling, biting my lip. I wouldn't let him see my fear.

'Come on,' he called, 'it's not cold. I won't let you drown.'

'No!' I said.

I looked across the dyke to the silvergreen tremble of the willows that grew on a far-away river bank. In the distance some people were working in a field. Small stooping figures. That was where the train ran over there, somewhere over there, the train to

Ely, the train perhaps to London. The place where Mother belonged.

They dragged this dyke but they could not find her. It was only that someone saw her stumbling forward one terrible night. He shouted but she did not hear. It was only that they found the flower from her hat, from her lovely hat, all wet and muddy near the edge.

'Come on, we must get back,' I said. 'They'll see that we're gone.'

Eventually he scrambled out, shivering, muddy from the bank. He pulled his clothes on over his damp skin and I noticed how black his feet were compared with the whiteness of his legs. His soles were hard as leather for he only wore boots in the winter. We did not talk as we walked back. He went before me, trying to whistle through chattering teeth. My mind was a tangle of different strings pulling all ways. I felt angry, almost jealous that Isaac had been in Mother's Dyke: I did not want to speak to him any more today. I also thought he was brave, because I *was* scared of that water. I also felt lonely already because I knew that soon he would go and then there would just be Aggie and Ellenanesther and me. And everything would be dull.

*   *   *

Aggie is nodding now, hands loosened on her knitting. It drops into her lap, her face sags. She snores softly. I can hear the twins in the kitchen; a moan from the cellar. What is the matter? He is dealt with for tonight. The moaning wakes Aggie. She jerks and then picks up her knitting, thinks I haven't noticed that there is a thin line of saliva on her chin, a dark spot of it on her chest.

'You've been dribbling,' I say, and she gives me her darkest look.

'Last night I had a dream,' she said. 'I dreamt about Father. Mother wasn't there, just Father. He was staring straight through me. I wasn't there at all.'

She goes back to her knitting. She's doing a complicated lacy pattern, like sea-shells, cockleshells. When we were girls we would dig shells up sometimes in the yard to give to Mother.

30

'I never dream of Father,' I say. 'But Mother is there, often. Not doing anything. Just there.'

I look at Aggie for a long time. Just an old woman, really a quite filthy old woman. Her grey hair is flat against her head with grease and the pink of her scalp gleams through. The deep lines on her face are filled with grime; her finger ends are brownish, the nails curved over like yellow claws.

'What are you staring at?' she says. I look away.

The pile of cats heaves and sighs as one extracts itself and goes towards the door. It stretches and sighs, yawns, and then looks at me expectantly. *Me*, though they are Agatha's cats, nothing to do with me. It gives me an insolent look. It is almost black in this shadowy gloom, its eyes are slits of light. I will not move, not for a cat, not to save Agatha the trouble. It goes behind Agatha's chair and I hear the dark hiss of its pee. The creature swaggers out, wiping its feet on the floor, and then relaxes into the furry pile, becomes indistinguishable among the tabby limbs.

'Filthy beasts,' I say to Agatha. I don't hold with animals in the house. 'Why don't you at least care for them properly, Agatha? Why don't you drown them?'

Agatha pretends not to hear. 'Such a terrible stench,' I add, though in truth it makes little difference. Agatha pulls a biscuit packet out from the side of her chair, a pink wafer packet. There are no more wafers left but she tips the crumbs into the palm of her hand, and licks them off. Disgusting.

'Imagine if we were to go into town,' she says, suddenly, dropping her knitting on the floor. 'Would you come? We could buy some new things. I could buy a new frock.' She stands up. She runs her hands over her scrawny body as if there is something worth showing off inside that old thing she wears, the colour of which is long forgotten beneath the splashes and stains of food and the cat hairs. Her hands rest on her hips. 'Blue has always suited me best,' she says. 'Of course on some it looks insipid. It takes a *complexion* to wear a proper blue.' She gives me a pitying look. 'And I will have my hair curled,' her hands describe a froth of curls around her head, 'and paint my nails. And shoes. Shoes with heels and pointed toes.' She tiptoes across the room, creaking and scattering biscuit crumbs, a stupid flirting look upon her face.

'And then we could go out to dinner. To a restaurant.' She sits down again. 'Imagine, Milly, a restaurant! With waiters, handsome waiters to wait on us hand and foot. What would we have, Milly?' she said.

'Oysters and beef,' I say, straining my memory for the details of luxury that mother taught us. 'And red wine and creme caramel.'

'And coffee *with* brandy!' she remembers. 'And chocolates!'

'And a swan carved out of ice. Mother told me about the swan carved out of ice, on a sea of violet petals.'

'Just to look at, not to eat,' adds Aggie. 'She told me, too.'

'She was out in a restaurant, eating dinner, with a man. Not Father.'

'Before she knew Father.'

'Swans of ice were not Father's sort of thing.'

'No,' says Aggie. She finishes licking between her fingers for the crumbs and picks up her knitting, but it has grown too dark to knit. In the kitchen Ellenanesther are muttering. I should go and see what they are doing, see that they are not playing with anything sharp. No. They're all right. They're fine. It does not do to meddle and I don't want to move, not quite yet. It's comfortable. It's growing chilly but I have made this chair warm and I do not want to leave the warmth, not just yet. It feels almost normal here. Two sisters, sitting of an evening, just talking, just reminiscing, like sisters do. Oh but it is such a mess! What ever would Mother have said?

'Perhaps, tomorrow, we should clear up?' I suggest, for I could not tackle it myself. She looks around the room and I follow her eyes. The corners have vanished now in shadows, but even so it is obvious that it is a hopeless task. The cats cover most of the floor and their hairs coat the carpet so that it is as soft and tabby as themselves. The hairs seem to float a little above the carpet, they sway as we move, they catch in the cobwebs, they are warm to walk in as warm water. Rubbish is everywhere. Mother's old piano is open and its keys are clogged with food and dust. They stay down if you press them. Sometimes, when the stove is lit we burn things, but more often, nowadays, they just stay where they are dropped. There are biscuit wrappers and paperbags and gin bottles and saucers encrusted with cat meat and cups clogged up with mould. We keep four cups clean, four plates, the cutlery and George's dish. That is sufficient. There are crumpled handkerchiefs and things the cats bring in and envelopes and, in here, there are the clothes left around my trunk. They have been on the floor since . . . since I decided to stay. That's when I stopped clearing up, when we all did. We just left everything, everything but the things we actually needed to use, just where it fell. It was a decision. Impressive. It was hard to stick to at first although it soon became a way of life. I cannot even tell what those things are now, the things it seemed so important for me, once, to take away from here. They are just lumps of soft grey dusty cloth. The only things that shine in this house are the mirrors. I rub them sometimes, just in the centre, to see my face, to see that I'm still here. Aggie looks more often. She preens like she's always done, always vain, though little good it's done her. I wonder what she sees. I do not think that it can be the truth.

The curtains reek of mould. You cannot touch them for they disintegrate at the slightest pull, showering mould spores in the air. It is all right in the summer. We want the light, and there is no need for privacy here. It will be cold in winter though. I do not want another winter.

'Remember Mrs Howgego,' I say, for tonight the past is on my mind more than ever.

'Remember Isaac, you really mean, dear.'

'Isaac too,' I agree.

'Oh Isaac,' she says, and sighs. I look at her sharply. 'He took a fancy to me, you know,' she says. Evil old bitch. Well I won't have it, not that, she's not poaching Isaac.

'Isaac was mine,' I say firmly, 'as you well know. Or have you gone completely doolally?'

'Only because he couldn't have me. I was far superior, he could see that, but I only had to snap my fingers, like so,' she snaps the bones of her old finger ends, 'and he would have come running.'

'Liar!' I say. 'Isaac would never have touched you, not with a bargepole he wouldn't. Not in a thousand years. He would never have touched you – because he *knew*.'

There is a gasp of cold silence, like the backwash of a wave. In all the time that has passed this has never been spoken. I watch Aggie's old face working, thinking, shrivelling. Despite the dark, she pretends to apply herself to her tight nylon shells. 'Yes, he did,' I continue, the urge to hurt her unbearable, irresistible, like an itch that will be scratched. 'He told me he knew. He asked me if it was true.'

'Whatever do you mean, dear? It's you that's doolally,' she says. She has made a decision. It will not come out. Well she hasn't got *all* the power.

'He said it was against the law. He said they would come and take you away, if they knew, to prison. He said it made him feel ill, you made him feel ill.' Aggie is trembling too much even to pretend to knit. 'I hate you Agatha!' I say. 'If it wasn't for you he would have married me. We would have got away . . .' I cannot prevent my voice rising to a wail. 'Away! I might have been away, far away. I might have been in London. I would have been Mrs Howgego . . . a grandmother by now perhaps. It was you Agatha. You ruined everything!'

My heart is beating hard; like a rat in a box it thumps, a strong thing, and I am breathless. I control my breathing and I close my eyes and only when I am calmer can I bear to look at Agatha again. I cannot see her expression because of the dark, but she is looking straight at me and she is calm. When she speaks there is relief in her voice.

'You lie,' she says. 'You are a liar. Isaac died before all that.'
She thinks she's got me. But I have tricked her.

'Before what then?' I say. 'Before what?'

She begins to hum in a cracked voice. I have never known anyone who could lie to herself like Agatha. I have hardly known anybody.

'I'll tell you what,' she says, in her important voice, 'Mark is bringing something new next time. Something new to try.'

She waits for me to ask – and I cannot help it. 'What sort of something new?'

'It's a special sort of food. Modern food. In a plastic pot. You pour water in and you get – oh all manner of things! Chinese food even! Rice and . . . oh all sorts. Dumplings I shouldn't wonder.'

'He's taken you for a fool, Agatha!'

'No. He told me all about them. You don't need a pan or a plate or anything. You just eat them from the pot.'

'Can't be much good.'

'They're delicious, he says. He practically lives on them, he says.'

'Anyway he will come tomorrow and we shall see.' Well, I am willing to try anything. You can't accuse *me* of narrow-mindedness.

Ellenanesther come through to say goodnight. They are old women, would seem old women to others, but to us they are still young. Still the babies. Their hair is grey now, long down their backs, cut in straight fringes like iron bars across their brows, but their faces are like children's faces, old and wrinkled dolls' faces. Flat, bland faces with big round eyes.

'Night night,' they say.

'Sleep tight, dears,' says Agatha.

'Watch that the bugs don't bite,' I say. Have said, for ever. Nonsense though, for the house is a swarm of bugs and fleas, the carpet jumping with them. Well, who's to say they haven't as much right here as ourselves? They'll be here long after we've gone. I read in a book that Mother gave me once, for Christmas, a natural history book, that there are insects, some insects, stag beetles or earwigs, perhaps, that can survive ice and fire. They'll be here long after we're gone, that's for sure.

Once Ellenanesther are safely upstairs I heave myself out of my chair, just to check the knives. They have polished them themselves. That is my job. They should not have done that. They should not play with the knives. However, they are all there, every one in its place. Neat. The knife drawer is the only neat place in the house, the knives and the mirrors the only things that shine.

Mother's kitchen is a terrible mess, a filthy mess. One day I'll clean it. I'll ask Mark to bring us scouring powder and if I search I'll find a brush and then I'll scrub the dirt away. Or perhaps I won't. Mark would be impressed if the kitchen was cleaned. I've seen the way he doesn't look at the awfulness, polite boy. His name is Mark Gotobed. He is the great-grandson of Sarah Gotobed who used to bring our groceries. I never liked her, but Mark, he is a fine boy. Mother would have approved, for he has manners.

*　　*　　*

Next time Mr Whitton brought his bull to serve Barley, I hung around. I didn't want to see – and I did. I wanted to know what Isaac knew. I tried chatting to Mr Whitton, not a chatty man, and certainly not bothered about passing the time of day with a little girl. He seemed uneasy, told me to run along. I went round the other side of Barley's stall and pretended I was not there.

'If there was any little girls in here, I'd tell them to buzz off,' said Mr Whitton, as if to the bull. 'Because I don't reckon they'd like seeing it. Not if they was good little girls they wouldn't.' I crouched silently down in the straw, my nose tickled and I was frightened I would sneeze. Mr Whitton muttered something more and then sighed. 'All right then,' he said. He dragged the hulk of a creature by the rope through the ring in its leathery nostrils into the stall. He goaded it a bit with a stick and pushed the gate shut behind it. I watched from behind my fingers, my eyes watering from the effort of not sneezing, the animal lump itself up onto poor old Barley's back. I could not breathe. I was sure that the weight of the brute would break her spine. I saw the wild look upon Barley's face, the way her eyes showed white and her tongue flickered sideways. The face of the bull was thick and expressionless. There was a hot meatish smell from it. I saw with horror the thick red rod of its thing.

My eyes were streaming and then it burst from me, a terrible noise half-way between a sneeze and a retch. I scrambled up out of the straw and bolted from the barn. I was thinking of Father and Mother. Imagining Father on Mother's back grunting and snorting, imagining Mother's frightened face and the awful thing going into her. I pelted out of the barn in an agony of embarrassment and revulsion.

'What's up with you?' Mr Whitton bellowed after me. 'Didn't you like it then?' I knew that he was laughing at my fear and I ran and ran from the barn, ran round the back of the house to the orchard and I was sick in the grass. Poor Mother. Poor poor Mother. And she had had to do it four times to get her children. Or three. Was it twice for twins? It was hateful and ugly and disgusting.

I climbed the apple tree, my special tree, and thought of Isaac, how I hated Isaac for knowing such a horrible disgusting thing all the time, and how he laughed as if it was some sort of joke. He laughed in the same way that Mr Whitton laughed, a man's way of laughing about a horrible man's thing. If staying nice meant not doing that then there was no danger for me. I thought that I would rather die.

I stayed in the apple tree a long time. I heard Mr Whitton and the beast leaving; I heard Aggie calling me once or twice and giving up. I sat still in the tree. I watched a kitten stalking in the grass; birds landed in the tree with me, so still was I; I saw a frog flopping in the grass towards the pond. Of course I didn't hate Isaac. But Mrs Howgego was right to call it not nice. But then if it was not nice, how did being married make it any nicer?

Ellenanesther came round the side of the house into the orchard. They were carrying something in a basket. They looked tiny from my perch in the tree, and charming really, a picture from a nursery rhyme with the sun shining on their brown hair, with their rosy faces and lashes that curved on their cheeks. They sat down close to my tree. They were muttering their own words, their funeral words: and the sonantheghost ohmothero anwaterandearth omotheromothero. They called the kitten that was playing in the grass, rustled their fingers at it, and it came to them, pink nose inquisitive, whiskers twitching. Then quickly, one of them snatched it up, and pushed it in the basket, and the other snapped down the lid. They went back round the house, out of sight, holding the basket between them, engrossed in their game.

I jumped from the tree and went back to the barn. Barley was there, chewing away, happy, quite happy, quite normal. It was all right then, perhaps.

*　　*　　*

It is my turn next. Aggie wouldn't dream of going upstairs before me – because she's the eldest. Always, Ellenanesther are first, and then me, and Aggie last of all.

In the kitchen I splash my face with water and then I make a trip to the privy. It rains still, pours from the sky, drenching, cool, refreshing. I stand for a moment feeling it trickle down my face, and then I walk away from the house to the little dark shed. It is hard to get into at this time of year for briars and brambles and honeysuckle and all sorts have clambered all over it. For a pee I just squat in the grass, usually, but tonight I have to stumble down the garden, feeling the wet scratch of ferns and wiry grass around my knees.

There is a stench in here, especially when it's been hot, but still, I like it. Once it was regularly scrubbed: brick floor; double wooden seat; and the light would float like bubbles through the knot holes in the door. It was fresh and clean, a good retreat – though freezing in the winter. I remember sitting on the seat with

Mother once, that was nice. She came with me because I was scared of what was down the hole. She sang a song as we sat there and I was never afraid again. There is a murmuring of flies underneath in the summer, and sometimes even the soft tap of one against my bottom. They are only flies though, they cannot harm me. And it is nice here. Some tendrils of clematis have forced their way in and there is even a luminous white flower just visible, just hovering.

I sit and listen to the noises of the night: the steady thrumming of the rain; scufflings in the grass, small creatures. There is a bird singing, a sweet liquid song it has. I don't know what it is. Nightingale? Blackbird? I've never learned. I have lived here for every minute of my life and yet I am not a country person. I do not know the details of the country. I am not at home here: will never be. I think if Mother had been a bird she would have been that sort of bird, with that sort of song.

Mother will keep coming into my head tonight. There is so much I don't know. If only she had lived longer; long enough to really talk to me, for me to understand. I still feel, old woman that I am, that I do not really understand. I understand almost nothing. What I know is like the skin on the surface of the water, glittering and rippling and reflecting, but underneath it is so deep and I do not know what is there.

My grandfather, Mother's father, was called Artie. He blacked his face with charcoal and sang upon the stage. A minstrel, he was, a real artiste, Mother said. She thought he was wonderful, but her mother disapproved. She had run away from her family and married him for love, and her rich and respectable family had cut her off without a penny. Washed their hands of her, Mother said, and I thought of the black charcoal, and I thought that I understood. Mother's mother had been a lady at heart, with very proper ways, and when the love wore off she was very bitter. She was angry with Artie for dragging her down, Mother said. She taught my mother to be a lady, to talk properly and to be polite. She tried to teach Mother that Artie was vulgar, but she never really believed that. She loved the songs and the music and the colours, and she loved her father who played with her and taught her songs instead of table manners; and stuck out his tongue and didn't frown at her. Mother taught us the manners and the way of speaking; she taught us to read and write a bit and count. She tried to teach us to play the piano, but only Aggie really had the knack. She taught us the songs too, and Aggie sings them still.

After Ellenanesther were born Mother cried a lot. One day when she was crying, I sat beside her and held her hand. She was sitting in her chair, the chair I like to sit on now – if Aggie doesn't get there first – and I sat on the wide arm of the chair and I held her hand which felt hot and thin and dry. 'Dear child,' she said, and then she started talking, telling me things, all in a jumble. She was crying and talking quickly and laughing too sometimes, and all the time she gripped my hand so tightly that I kept the prints of her fingers for hours. That was when she told me about the ice swan and the violet petals, a sea of violet petals upon the snowy tablecloth. She was dining with a man; and they had oysters and beef and creme caramel. And her long black hair was piled up upon her head and she wore glittering jewels and her dress was emerald green and low in the front, and her skin was white and perfect. She must have looked beautiful; and I was proud that she talked to me so much and held on to me so tight – but I was frightened too. And it was another man, not Father, it was just before she met Father. And she loved this man – I do not even know his name – and she thought that he would marry her. She said she wished that he could have seen Agatha, could have seen what a beauty she had turned out to be. And I minded that. Why Agatha and why not me?

I wish I knew why he didn't marry Mother. I *wish* I knew. I do not even know his name. She was so beautiful, my mother, and so funny and so loving. How could he *not* have wanted to marry her, with the swan of ice and the emerald dress and all?

There was another thing about Mother, she could sing, really

40

sing. Her voice was like . . . like stars and crisp apples and cool water. Oh . . . it was like a smile. It made you smile inside, a warm tickle in your belly. She knew so many songs too; sweet ones and sad ones and love songs and funny songs; and she could speak in all sorts of different voices, mimic people and make us fall off our stools with laughing. Oh Mother. Oh how I miss you still.

She nearly was a singer. If she hadn't married Father she would have been. She said, 'I could have managed, Milly. I had my voice. I didn't need to marry, not really, but it seemed the only way. I didn't want to disgrace my mother. It would have killed her. It seemed the only way, when your father turned up out of the blue like that and proposed, promised to take me away. It seemed the only way out.'

I was only a little girl and I did not understand. It was no use her talking to me, ignorant little wretch that I was. I just held her hand while she talked, and thought about the ice swan, and I did not understand.

I am getting cold, sitting here. There is something in here with me, a mouse or something like. The cats will be out soon to hunt them. They bite the heads off them: mice and voles, rats, birds, even small rabbits – and they bring them into the kitchen – gifts for Aggie. I hate to see the baby birds. It upsets me when they bring in baby birds, for they are so ugly – bulbous blue organs in distorted pink sacs. They make me feel sick. I wish they wouldn't bring those in.

Tomorrow Mark will come with another bottle of gin and all the rest. A jar of olives for me, the green ones stuffed with red. Aggie hates them now though she craved them once, and I eat them all myself. I am intrigued by the idea of these meals that come in their own pots, to which you only have to add water. Chinese too! Whatever next!

'That's me done,' I say to Aggie who has been sitting in the dark waiting. She pushes her needles through her squeaky wool, and waits for me to say my line. I could upset her by not saying it, by saying something else, but I don't.

'Goodnight. Sleep tight. Watch that the bugs don't . . .'

'Bite. Sweet dreams.' She angles her face up to me and I bend down and brush the withered softness of her cheek with my lips. This is our only touching.

At last it is really night. All I have to do now is get under my blanket and listen to Agatha talking to her cats, bidding them good hunting; and then she stumps stiffly and creakily up the two flights of stairs to her room. Once she is quiet, I am free. There are hours and hours of night and I can think what I like, remember what I like, without Aggie getting in the way.

The rain still pours and George is noisy tonight, strangely noisy. His groans will intrude upon my night. No cellar is deep enough, far enough, to allow us to forget George.

The best nights are the nights when I remember Isaac, when it all comes back, all the good times when I was a little girl with a friend, and then a young woman. On the worst nights Father lurks, thoughts of Father and George are there in the shadows waiting for me to become unwary, waiting to slide into my head.

I hardly sleep any more. I have forgotten how. I suppose I slide into a doze now and then – but I do that all the time. I don't have a set time to sleep and a set time to wake like real people. All day I stay downstairs and I am awake and half awake and then I doze and then I wake; and in the night, upstairs, it is the same. Sometimes the states merge into one, like a half-waking dream, pictures of the past flickering transparently upon the wreck of the present.

There goes Aggie again, bang and crash and scrape. Where she gets the energy from I don't know. I can hear her pacing. I can hear her sighing. Why must she always sigh? I swear I can hear her sighing, even from here.

Oh I don't like the noises tonight. I do not think it will be a good night. The rain streams down, and Agatha paces, and

George moans and the cats are howling – and there is another noise. I do not want to think. Do not think. Think about something else. Something else. Something nice. Oh I shall go mad. Think about something nice.

*   *   *

One hot cloudless summer's morning, Mother packed food into a basket. 'I have a plan,' she said. 'We're going for a picnic.'

'Hoorah!' I shouted. 'Shall we have ham? Shall we have currant cake and lemonade?'

'Hush,' laughed Mother. 'You must wait and see.'

Agatha ran to the mirror to look at her face, and to smooth her hair. 'Do I look nice, Mother? Shall we be seeing anyone?'

'Well . . . first I thought it could just be us. But I'd like a word with Mrs Howgego so I thought we might walk that way. She might like to join us. Then Milly could play with Isaac. Would you like that, Milly?'

'Oh yes!'

'But Mother . . .' said Agatha.

'But what?' she demanded.

'But Father wouldn't like . . . I thought . . . I mean Mrs Howgego isn't exactly . . .'

'My darling little snob,' said Mother in a hard new voice that we had never heard before, 'your father has some funny ideas, but what he doesn't know won't hurt him.'

'But that's lies!' I exclaimed, thrilled.

'No, it's not lies,' said Mother more gently. 'We know that Mrs Howgego – and Isaac – are nice. They are our friends. Your father doesn't understand, doesn't understand how lonely it gets out here. He won't know unless we tell him. If he asked, if he actually asked, "Did you go on a picnic with the Howgegos," you'd have to say yes, otherwise it would be a lie. But it's not a lie if he doesn't know anything about it. Anyway,' she added less convincingly, 'I'm sure he wants us to have fun. It will be fun, won't it?'

We nodded.

'It'll make us happy.'

'Yes.'

'It won't hurt anyone. It won't hurt him.'

'No.'

'Well then, let's get going!'

Mrs Howgego looked at the mountain of grey sheets and shirts on the floor.

'They'll wait,' persuaded Mother. 'Come on Candida . . . it's a lovely day . . .'

'Go on, Mam,' said Isaac.

'Please,' I said.

'Oh all right,' said Mrs Howgego. 'This lot's waited long enough, another day won't hurt . . .' Mrs Howgego didn't have a proper time to do things like Mother who always got the washing out of the way on Monday so that Tuesday was spent in the steamy heat of the iron. 'You two get round the back and pick us some of them raspberries and redcurrants,' she said, thrusting a bowl at Isaac. Holding hands, we ran outside joyously and ate more than we saved and returned to the kitchen with red-stained lips and fingers.

'That's your share then,' said Mother smartly. I didn't care. I could see Mrs Howgego's bulging baskets of food waiting beside Mother's on the floor, and I shrugged carelessly. Mother laughed. 'What a little piglet you are!'

Agatha flung me a scornful glance from her slim height.

'Let's not go too far,' I begged. I was hungry for all the lovely things in store. 'My feet are aching already.'

'Just to the dyke,' promised Mother. 'I'll tell you what, Candida, let's walk along the dyke to the trees. It's not much further, and then we can sit in the shade.'

Davey and Bobby came too, Davey riding on Isaac's shoulders. I dawdled behind, watching, knowing that I must pay attention, that I must store up these happy moments in my head. Agatha walked ahead as always, slim and straight, carrying the smallest of the baskets; Mother and Mrs Howgego followed, both heavily laden, little Bobby dangling from Mrs Howgego's skirts, their heads bent towards each other, deep in conversation. Isaac followed, a slim reed of a boy, swaying with the weight of the fat baby balanced on his shoulders. There was a happiness surrounding us all, a holiday feeling that you could almost see.

It wasn't far to the dyke from the Howgegos' house. We walked further along than usual, to a shady copse of willows, and soon we were spreading Mother's large old red and white spotted cloth on the ground. Agatha tried to arrange the food artistically but the baby kept crawling across and putting his fingers into everything; and I could not control myself and kept picking the crusty bits off the end of the bread.

The sun was hot but there was a bit of a breeze and the willows rippled shadows across our chosen spot. It was a perfect place, a little hollow by the side of the dyke where the baby could crawl safely and our mothers lean themselves back in comfort and talk.

There was silence at first, except for the chewings and the slurpings. There was cold sausage pie and pickled onions and walnuts; and fresh bread and butter and cheese; there was quince jam and bramble jelly and raspberry buns and honey buns and currant cake. There was a bottle of cold tea, and lemonade, and Mrs Howgego's ginger beer, a warm, flat friendly drink. I could never again taste ginger beer without thinking of this day; this picnic by the dyke, with Isaac and Mother.

We ate till we could hardly move. 'Tuck in,' Mrs Howgego kept saying. 'What's left will all have to be carried back.' Even I came to a full-stop in the end, and had to lie still for ten minutes to let it all go down a bit. Agatha, who, it was said, ate like a bird, wandered about along the top of the dyke, picking the odd flower and singing the songs she wasn't allowed to sing when Father was home and her true voice drifted down so we caught the odd snatch:

She sang like a nightingale, twanged her guitar;
Danced the cachuca and smoked a cigar;
Oh what a form! Oh what a face!

'*She did the fandango all over the place!*' joined in Mother.

Mrs Howgego laughed. 'And she do sing like a nightingale, that girl,' she said. Agatha had drifted away again.

'Yes . . . she does,' said Mother, 'she's got a lovely voice.'

I struggled up from the ground. I had better things to do than stay and hear them praising Aggie. 'Come on,' I said. Isaac was lying on his back, the shadows making complex patterns on his freckly face. I poked him with my toe. 'Come on, lazy oaf.'

'Milly!' exclaimed Mother, 'language!'

'Oh leave the girl alone,' said Mrs Howgego. 'I reckon she's right.'

Isaac jumped up. 'Race you then,' he said, already darting off, 'then we'll see who's a lazy oaf.' I charged after him although I knew there was no chance of catching him up, and Bobby followed.

'Go back to Mam,' said Isaac breathlessly, when he'd beaten me fair and square and we were lying on the grass recovering.

'No, Zac, wanna play with you,' said Bobby, his lip jutting out ready to cry.

'You're too small,' complained Isaac.

'Mam told me to come and play with you.'

'Look!' I cried pointing at something snaky moving in the grass.

'That's a slow-worm,' said Isaac. 'If I catch him for you Bob, will you go away and play?'

'Yup,' said Bobby fervently. 'I want him.'

Isaac shot out his hands and caught the creature. I shuddered. I wasn't squeamish and girlish about spiders and frogs but couldn't stand anything long and wriggly. It was about six inches long, a greyish bronze thing, a long lashing muscle with tiny bright eyes.

'Want to have a look Milly?'

'Don't like snakes,' I dared to say.

'Snakes!' said Isaac. 'He's not a snake! Here.'

He waved it at me and I backed away.

'Look Bob,' said Isaac, 'I reckon she's afraid of him, little ittybitty slow-worm.'

'I'm not afraid. I just don't like them,' I said firmly.

'Prove it then,' said Isaac. 'Prove you int afraid. Hold him.'

'Go on, Milly,' urged Bobby, 'then I can have him.'

With pretended indifference, I held out my hand. It won't hurt. It's only little, I thought, willing my hand not to shake. He wouldn't give it me if it would hurt. Not with Mother so near, and his mam.

'Are you sure it won't bite me?'

'I'm not 'fraid, am I, Zac?' said Bobby proudly.

The creature slithered on my hand, warm and dry. 'Mind out, you'll drop him!' said Isaac, and sure enough the slow-worm dropped from my flattened palm. I could not make myself grasp it.

'Catch him Zac!' shrieked Bobby. Isaac leapt forward and scooped it up again.

'What's the matter with you then?' he asked.

'Nothing,' I said.

'Oh come on,' he said. 'Don't put that face on. I was only teasing.'

'Let's climb trees then,' I suggested. This was the thing that I could do as well as Isaac. 'That's a good one, there.' There was a big old sycamore with wide hospitable branches among the willows in the copse where we'd been sitting.

'Let's creep up so no one sees us,' said Isaac.

We reached the trees with no one seeing, and on the far side of the trunk, we scrambled up. It was a tall tree, much taller than the apple tree in the garden. Its branches were broad and strong and full of ragged leaves which tickled my face as I lay full length on my belly, gazing at the scene below.

'They haven't seen us,' I whispered to Isaac, who perched slightly above me. 'Can you see Agatha?'

'I reckon she's gone soft in the head!' said Isaac and we giggled so that the branches shook and threatened to dislodge us; for Agatha, believing that she was out of sight, was acting away to an imaginary audience, wagging her finger and gesticulating along with her song.

'We're like spies,' said Isaac, when Agatha's antics had ceased to amuse us.

'Yes. We can see what everyone's doing – and they can't see us. Look at Bobby!' Bobby was wriggling and squirming, a mysterious smile on his face.

'He's got that slow-worm down his pants I reckon,' said Isaac. I shuddered. 'What is it then if it's not a snake?' I asked.

'Shhh,' hissed Isaac, 'if you stop yakking for a minute, we can hear what they're saying.'

I strained my ears. It was true that if you listened carefully and concentrated hard to sift the soft speech from the rustling of the leaves, you could just hear snatches of the conversation between Mother and Mrs Howgego.

'That's boring,' I complained. 'Who wants to listen?'

'Shhh,' commanded Isaac again.

I sighed and relaxed, wondering whether it would be possible to fall asleep here, pressed against this strong, slightly swaying branch. I was still full, and the sun filtered warm through the leaves. I didn't share Isaac's interest in eavesdropping, but unwillingly my ears began to focus in on the conversation below us.

'I know,' Mother was saying, 'but I do hope it's a boy this time. Charles has never . . . well he loves little Milly of course, his image, but Aggie . . .'

'Who is *your* image.'

'He's never really taken to Aggie.' This was news to me. I always thought everyone doted on Agatha.

'And do you think he knows?'

'He's never said, but yes, I think he's realized. He's different with Milly, you see. He's all right with Aggie – but just not like a father. And his temper gets worse.'

'Oh Phylly,' said Mrs Howgego, 'and is he still. . . ?'

'I'm not so afraid now that I'm expecting again. He's so careful about this son I'm supposed to be having.'

'I didn't know she was expecting!' I hissed indignantly.

'I know what I'd like to do to that husband of yours,' said Mrs Howgego darkly.

'And you will be there?' said Mother, clutching Mrs Howgego's hand. 'I don't know what I'd do without you, Candida. It's been so awful.'

'I'm getting down,' I said, feeling suddenly sick on the swaying branch. I scrambled down the tree, and Isaac, in one light leap, landed beside me. 'I'm going to walk along the dyke,' I said, and strode off pretending not to care whether he followed or not. My face was burning. What did she mean?

The surface of the water reflected the sky, a blue metallic sheen over its muddiness. I gazed down into it. 'What did she mean?' I demanded of Isaac who stood meekly at my shoulder. 'What did your mother mean about my father?'

Isaac shrugged. 'Well he belts her, doesn't he? I reckon that's what she means.'

'Belts her! No never,' I said. I hurried away from him but he followed close behind.

'I heard them talking about it before,' he said, as if this would comfort me. 'That's nothing new. My dad belts my mam too. She do belt him back though,' he added thoughtfully. 'I can't see your mam doing that.'

'But . . .' But a hundred muffled cries and sharply closing doors; a hundred fearful expressions, blinked back tears, bruises, cuts; a hundred things to be kept from Father – songs and laughter, friends, this very day. A thousand unexplained things fell into place with a horrifying jangle.

I looked Isaac straight in the eye. 'There's one more thing I don't understand,' I said. 'What did Mother mean about Aggie?'

Isaac's eyes slid back to the water. 'Let's go and see if there's any ginger beer left,' he said.

'Isaac,' I insisted, catching hold of his arm. 'You must tell me if you know. I must know.' Isaac sat down, dangling his dirty toes above the moving surface of the water. 'Please,' I said.

Isaac hesitated, then he looked accusingly at me. 'That's not fair,' he said, 'whenever I tell you something you don't like,' his eyes looked searchingly into mine, 'you get mad at me.'

'Oh I don't!'

'Oh yes you do, Milly. That's all right when we're playing games and such like but then I go and say something and you get mad at me.'

'Well,' I said, 'I still have to know. You have to tell me.'

Isaac threw a lump of dried earth into the water. It made a fat plopping sound as it sank out of sight, and we watched the circles it made vanishing into the flow of the water. 'I'm not sure,' he said. 'I reckon I know what she meant but I'm not sure.'

'Yes?'

'That Aggie has a different dad.'

'What do you mean!' This was too preposterous. 'How can she? Mother's married to Father, to our father. You must have got it wrong.' I relaxed. For once Isaac didn't know it all. For once he was wrong. It made me like him more then, his pale worried face, his serious voice. And he was wrong.

Isaac looked at me, a wry smile on his face. 'Yes,' he said, relieved, 'I reckon I got it wrong.'

'Come on then,' I said, pulling him up, 'let's go and get a drink.'

* * *

How long will the house last? It's an old house. A good square house, but an old one. We haven't done the things you're meant to do: painting and papering and plastering. It would mean cleaning first. Those things come after cleaning. When things drop we leave them where they fall. When things break we leave them broken. The house is older than us. We will die: the house will fall down. And that will be a finish.

There are broken windows and missing roof tiles. A gutter has peeled away from the roof at the back, and swung out, tangling with the fruit trees. Good trees they are, they haven't been pruned for . . . well years, not for tens of years and still in the autumn there are apples and pears and, some years, a crop of sticky golden plums. We have to fight the wasps for the plums. The noise I can hear is like wasps, a waspish noise, a low buzzing murmur, dangerous. Don't think about it. Don't think.

Mark's father was looking for odd jobs, so Mark said. Would we like him to fix the gutter? Replace the glass in the windows? Take a look at the roof? We said no, Agatha and I, we agreed. She gets letters full of numbers from the bank sometimes, in envelopes with little windows that tell her that there is enough money still for groceries, just, but nothing else. Besides, there seems little point. We are all right like this. There is a satisfaction in watching the house grow old along with us.

A young woman came to visit us some time ago. She came several times, oh some time back now. She was from Social Services she said.

'You've come to the wrong place here,' I said. 'We're not very social.'

'That's just why I'm here, Miss Pharoah,' she said, *so* polite. Mark's mother who is some sort of a busybody, well it runs in the Gotobed family, had contacted somebody or other when Mark told them what a mess our house is, I shouldn't wonder. 'It's a mystery to us. It's almost as if – as far as the authorities and so on are concerned – you don't exist. It's not being on a road, I suppose, or connected to any mains services.' She had her hair very short and she wore great big spectacles with green frames. Green! And she wore wonderful clothes. Red trousers, tight, and a sort of baggy, I can only describe it as a vest, but a lovely one, yellow with a pattern on it. She did look cheerful.

'And we don't seem to have you on any of our GPs' lists.'

'GPs?'

'Doctors.'

'Oh we can't be doing with doctors.'

'But you must . . . you're getting on all of you . . . you must have a doctor. You never know what might happen.'

'We might drop dead,' I said.

She was nervous, I realized, with her little eyes blinkety blinkety behind those great lenses, and her chewed-up fingernails. And she wasn't any prettier than I used to be. And she had tiny parrots hanging from her ears! She said there were places we could go to be looked after. We could still be quite independent, she said, with our own front door, and our own key, only there would be a warden to keep an eye on us, a bell to ring in an emergency. Well we have our own front door, thank you very much, I told her, though the key went missing a long time since; and an emergency is just what we need – then that would be an end of it. All of us were born in this house, and in this house we intend to die.

Sometimes when there's a storm, when the wind roars and blunders around the house, I think that it will simply fall down and bury us. That would be neat, a tidy end. I wonder how long before anyone noticed? The briars and the brambles would simply grow over the ruins, the beams; the bones; the old sticks of furniture and our four skulls. The cats would prowl, would eat our flesh, would eat the rats that came to gnaw our bones. I have no illusions about the cats – unlike Agatha.

*   *   *

One November morning when the wind growled round the house, when it was not yet light except for a seam of sickly yellow that showed on the horizon through the black filth of a Fen blow, Mother sat with her back pressed to the stove, her hands clasped round her distended belly, rocking herself gently backwards and forwards.

Father stood before her, dressed to go to town. He looked smart and handsome and fine.

'Charles no . . . the girls . . .' whimpered Mother. She looked up at him, beseechingly, and her face was swollen and wet.

I was on my way downstairs, my head full of stories and dreams, and I stopped, unnoticed, half-way down. I stood and watched my father tread, with his hard shiny black shoe, on my mother's softly slippered foot. He trod hard, grinding his heel.

I saw my mother's face, the way the tears flowed over bruises. I saw my father step back off my mother's foot. I saw my mother close her eyes, and wrap her arms tightly around herself and press back against the warmth of the stove. I saw my father strike my mother sharply on the belly with his malacca cane. 'Bastard,' I heard him say. 'Another bastard for me to feed. You fucking whore.' And then he left.

I could not bear to see the tears seeping from Mother's eyes. I did not know what I could do or say. I did not understand. I crept back up the stairs and into bed. I put my head under my pillow and I held my breath, and I tried to die.

*   *   *

I remember the afternoon the twins were born. Father was away and Mrs Howgego was upstairs with Mother. Aggie had run over in the morning and asked her to come. Isaac and I had to mind Bobby and Davey. I wasn't allowed upstairs in Mother's bedroom, but Aggie was, for whenever Mrs Howgego needed something – hot water, cool water, clean sheets – she'd call Agatha. And Agatha thought she was *so* important. She hardly glanced at me. Oh there was such a high and mighty look upon her face. She might have been making trips to heaven the way she looked.

At least Isaac was with me. We sat by the window, not talking, just looking out at the dreadful day – it was almost dark by half-past three. A dirty rain beat against the windows and occasional drops of it sizzled down the chimney onto the fire that just would not burn properly. When the wind's in a particular direction it never will, and on this day there was more smoke than flame and when the wind gusted it blew puffs of it back down the chimney and into the room.

Davey was toddling about, pulling down everything he could reach, opening cupboards and pulling out the contents, making a terrible mess everywhere; and Bobby had brought a wet half-grown cat in from outside and was teasing it so that it clawed its way up the curtains and knocked things off the shelves.

And in the background always, from above us, I could hear Mother moaning with pain.

I knew she would hate the mess and the noise. I knew I should make it tidy and quiet; make the boys behave; make the fire burn bright; the rain stop; the pain stop. I felt useless.

There was at last a cry that covered me in goose-flesh and brought frightened tears jumping to my eyes. And then it was quiet. I didn't even think of the baby, so relieved was I that Mother's pain had stopped. And then as if in a nightmare, it began again.

'Aggie!' shouted Mrs Howgego, and Agatha shot up the stairs as if she'd been fired from a catapult. She struggled down a few minutes later with a basin full of bloody water.

'More water, try and find some more sheets . . . It's a girl and it looks like there's another.' She emptied the bowl and refilled it with clean water from the kettle, then she refilled the kettle and set it back on the stove. So busy and clever and useful. I felt like a worm.

'Sheets!' she hissed at me. 'And would you pump some more water.'

'Twins then,' said Isaac, when Agatha had gone back upstairs.

'Maybe the other one will be a boy,' I said, not caring, but knowing that that was what Mother wanted. If not, Father might be even more angry, two more girls' mouths to feed. 'Bastards,' I whispered.

'What?' said Isaac.

'Oh nothing.' I felt sick. I did not want to know any more today.

*

Once, when I was very young, I had come across one of the cats in the barn while she was kittening. I had not, at first, realized what was happening. I had almost tripped over her in the barn, among the scattered straw. I thought at first that she was injured, trodden on by Barley perhaps. She lay on her side, face twitching, tail lashing wildly, howling and growling if I tried to come nearer. I watched the first of the births not understanding, thinking at first, horrified, that it was part of her own injured body that was squeezing out of her. And then I understood, saw that the knobbly bluish bundle was a kitten. I watched the cat turn and nip and rip the creature free from its skin bag and the long twisted string attached to its belly; and then lick the blind and sticky thing until it mewed, a thin high mew. And then it started again, the howling and the growling and there was another birth and another until there were six.

I told Mother about the new kittens, and Aggie heard and was angry. 'Why didn't you call me!' she said. She liked to be there when the cats kittened, in case they needed help. She found it fascinating and wonderful, not like me. I found it quite interesting – but more disgusting.

'Don't tell your father there are any more kittens,' Mother had warned.

'Or he'll murder them,' I said.

'He'll want them drowned,' she agreed. 'We're getting overrun.'

'Never!' Aggie had cried in her most dramatic of voices. 'If Father drowns them I'll run away! I'll never come back.'

'There's no need for that,' Mother had replied. 'With any luck he won't notice.'

I could not stand to hear Mother in pain. It had seemed so easy for the cat, but it was not the same for Mother. It took so long. All I could worry about was the mess. I was so worried about the mess in the room! I suppose I thought she'd be down when she'd finished to cook the tea, cross with me for not keeping things clean and neat. I was an ignorant child. I would not look at Isaac. No doubt he knew all about it, things that I didn't. No doubt he was noticing how useless I was while Agatha knew just what to do.

Eventually, Mrs Howgego came down the stairs. She looked tired and white and the front of her apron was red with blood. My mother's blood.

'Will you get that kettle on again and make me a cup of tea, Milly?' she said, flopping exhausted into a chair. I'd never seen her like that before.

'Is my mother all right?'

'Your mam is . . . very tired,' she said gently. 'Sometimes when ladies have babes they get very tired and they bleed a lot. She's had a terrible time. I was all of a mind to send Isaac to the village for the doctor, but she wouldn't have it. She's very torn and ever so weak. But I reckon she'll be all right now. She'll have to rest up. You'll have to be good girls and help out. You've got two new little sisters,' she added, 'no bigger than this.' She held her hands a few inches apart.

'Can I see?' I asked.

'I should leave them be.'

'Please . . .' surprising myself, I burst suddenly into tears. I needed to see my mother. I didn't even care if Isaac saw me crying. 'I want my mother!'

'Oh all right then,' said Mrs Howgego, 'I don't suppose that'll hurt. But don't you go pestering her, and don't wake her if she's asleep. You just take her up a cup of tea and leave it by the bed.'

I fumbled with the pot, shooting tea everywhere with my trembling hands. Mother was torn. I expected to find her lying like a tatty bloody rag on the bed – but no – I opened the door with one hand, cup and saucer rattling dangerously in the other, and there was Mother. She looked just the same as usual, only very pale and very small. She was tucked into clean sheets, her dark, damp hair brushed away from her creamy brow, her eyes closed. I was relieved that I could see no blood.

I put the cup down gently beside her and she opened her eyes. 'Milly,' she whispered, 'there's a good girl.'

'Are you all right now?' I asked, bending to kiss her cheek. For a moment it felt as if I was the mother and she was the child, small and needy, tucked up in bed.

'Yes, I'm all right now,' she whispered, but her voice was papery thin. 'There are your new sisters,' she said, and nodded to the old crib at the end of the bed.

They looked like skinned rabbits, little red wizened faces, heads no bigger than apples, hands the size of halfpennies.

'Are they all right?' I asked.

'I think so,' said Mother, 'but they're very small. They've come too early. We'll have to keep them very warm.'

There was a funny smell about Mother, an ill, animally sort of smell that was stronger than the lavender smell of her soap.

'I'm going to drink this lovely cup of tea you've brought me,' she said, 'and then I'm going to have a little sleep.' I could see that her eyelids were fluttering already. 'Be a good girl and thank Mrs Howgego, won't you.'

'Yes, I will,' I promised. I would have done anything then to help Mother, to make her happier and stronger, but the smell made me feel sick and the sight of the babies who had hurt her so much made me feel sick too. 'See you later on,' I whispered, 'I'll bring you some food when you wake up.' I crept out of the room and closed the door softly behind me.

*   *   *

I do not like the noises in this house tonight. It is not just George, it is not just those awful howls; it is not even the sound of Aggie pacing about, dragging something about; it is the other noise that is the worst.

It is Ellenanesther I can hear. It is their voices I can hear, their language of half words, nonsense words, muttering and mumbling and buzzing through the walls. It seems to vibrate inside the bricks of the house, to shake the walls and the ceilings. They are mad and they are dangerous, yet we live with them, have lived with them all our lives and been all right.

Pretty faces they have still, like pushed-in doll faces, and they wear their iron hair in straight bars across their foreheads and hanging long down their backs. And sometimes they wear ribbons

*   *   *

After the twins were born, Mother kept to her bed for a long time. The birth of Ellenanesther did something to her, shrunk her somehow, diminished her, and that part of her never quite grew back. Father mainly stayed away. Oh he did come back from time to time, and when he came back he was kinder than he'd been lately. On the surface he seemed kind, but I knew, thought I knew, thought I had seen – or had I dreamed? – his cruelty to Mother. Aggie was charmed. Hung around him, grateful for every word he spoke, every breath he breathed in this house. There was Mother upstairs and it was as if Aggie was grateful. She could play the woman of the house now, with Mother tucked away safely like a sickly child. She could make Father's tea just the way he liked it, and jump up to pour him a second cup before he'd even swallowed the last of his first.

Poor Mother, little white face against the pillow, little thin white hands. I was angry with her for being weak. She was supposed to be my mother, to be strong. I couldn't stand the tears that crept out from the corners of her closed eyes.

'What's the matter, Mother?' I would say. 'When are you getting up?' And sometimes, looking at Father's calm and handsome face in the firelight I used to wonder if it was her fault and not his. Perhaps it was Mother's fault that this was not a happy home. There she lay growing whiter and whiter as if the pair of wailing skinned rabbits were sucking her blood from her and not just her milk. Why couldn't she just get up now and be our mother, properly our mother again? It made me so angry to hear her trembly tearful voice. Oh she was tired for the babies cried all night. I used to hear her moving about, pacing, sometimes singing and sometimes crying herself and yet in the morning they all slept, and we had to tiptoe and whisper our way through our work. Sometimes I felt I would have liked to hit her myself, just to get her moving, wake her up.

But Father stayed away most of the time. He had too much work. And the weather was too bad for him to travel home more often, he said. I don't suppose there was much to come back for. Only us, little girls, and a sick wife and a pair of babies that kept him awake and in which he showed not the slightest interest. I saw him, I saw the way he averted his eyes from them and I couldn't blame him for they were ugly and noisy and squirmy.

Mrs Howgego came to visit once a week or so, and helped us with the house. She always brought some food with her to warm up in our oven, and in an hour or so she'd get the place feeling right again. I do not understand even now the sort of magic she had. She was not a tidy or a methodical person but she had a way of poking the fire that brought it leaping to life; and she could, just by moving a chair a fraction, sweeping the table free of clutter and straightening the hearth rug, make it feel right and safe, bring a sense of order into the room.

I remember a time close to Christmas. The babies were still tiny, but stronger now and we had brought them downstairs and tucked them in their crib by the fire. Aggie and I had decorated a little branch from outside and put it on the shelf over the hearth with some new candles. With the fire blazing, and the timid white dance of the candle flames; with the warm smell of Mrs Howgego's pie in the oven and her Christmas present to us, a fat cake bursting with fruit, on the table, the room looked lovely.

And then Mother came down. 'That's about time, Phyll,' I heard Mrs Howgego saying to her sternly. 'You won't feel any better stuck up here. You come down and start getting things shipshape again. Those poor girls of yours need their mam. You're no more use than ornament stuck away up here.'

And Mother, pale and frail but obedient, came downstairs and sat on the chair by the fire. The firelight brought a glow to her cheeks and she held a cup of tea between her palms and I thought it would be all right. We all drank tea, and then Isaac came in, his nose like a cold cherry, with his Christmas present to us: a basket of chestnuts he'd picked and saved.

I do remember that afternoon close to Christmas, with Mother back downstairs, and Mrs Howgego and Isaac, and the firelight dancing on the walls and then the smell of roasting chestnuts and the dry burnt taste of the shells on my teeth and finally the hot chewy sweet nuts inside. I felt complete then, but sad too because I knew this would not last. I was nostalgic already for this moment. I could not really immerse myself in it, rather hold back and watch and save it up because I knew that soon Isaac and Mrs Howgego would go. I knew that then the babies would wake and wail and that Mother would have no time for us and that the fire would go down. It would grow chilly and gloomy and Mother might weep. I wanted to tie a string around everyone and keep them there, prisoners of this moment, when everything was as it should be.

But, of course, I was right and it all dissolved. When the Howgegos opened the door to leave, the cold and the damp leapt in like cats, and the babies woke. The candles drowned in their own tears and the fire sulked. Father was expected home and Aggie and I struggled to make things tidy, to clear the mess of chestnut shells from the hearth, while Mother nursed the wailing twins.

Mother did not return to bed. Once Mrs Howgego had persuaded her to get up she stayed up, but she remained pale, like a watery reflection of herself. Aggie and I got used to it. I always felt angry when she sank weakly down in a chair, when she sighed so wearily. I pretended not to see, not like Aggie. She was there with cups of tea, and a stool for Mother's feet and a cushion for her back. She loved it, loved to be strong while Mother was weak, and Mother thought she was wonderful. 'Oh Agatha,' she'd say in her trembly voice, 'you are an angel.' And Agatha would gloat, and I would pretend not to have noticed, not to have heard.

Father stayed away more and more, even when the weather improved and there was not so much excuse. Sometimes, just sometimes, as spring approached and freed us, little by little, from the pull of the hearth, glimpses of our old mother would return. She might sing to us and joke and there was a warm feeling about us like there used to be. One day, after Mrs Howgego had left, Agatha kept asking Mother why it was that Father didn't approve of her, didn't like Mother being friends with her, why they had to keep it a secret. 'Is it because she's common and poor?' she asked. 'Because she's so fat and her dress is all patched?'

Mother was quiet for a moment, looking hard at Agatha until she looked down, embarrassed. I thought she would be angry with Agatha. I hoped she would be angry, but instead she just smiled sadly. 'That is part of it, yes,' she said. 'Father doesn't understand, like we do, that Mrs Howgego is a saint. Those things, the clothes and the money, are not important. It's what's inside that's important.' She hugged Agatha. 'My mother taught me a rhyme when I was just your age,' she said. 'Let me see if I can remember it.' She gazed into the fire, the dark little furrow of a frown on her forehead. I thought of Mrs Howgego's face, her little bright blue eyes and the purple squiggles in her fat cheeks. Mrs Howgego the saint. 'I remember!' she said and she stood by the window, her hands clasped together, exactly like a little girl, and she recited the rhyme. ' "Vulgar Little Lady," ' she said and cleared her throat and began.

' "But mamma now," said Charlotte, "pray don't you
     believe
That I'm better than Jenny my nurse?
Only see my red shoes and the lace on my sleeve;
Her clothes are a thousand times worse.

I ride in my coach and have nothing to do,
And the country folk stare at me so;
And nobody dares to control me but you,
Because I'm a lady you know.

Then, servants are vulgar, and I am genteel;
So really 'tis out of the way,
To think that I should not be better a deal
Than maids and such people as they."

"Gentility, Charlotte," her mother replied,
"Belongs to no station or place;
And nothing's so vulgar as folly and pride,
Though dress'd in red slippers and lace.

Not all the fine things that fine ladies possess
Should teach them the poor to despise;
For 'tis in good manners, and not in good dress,
That the truest gentility lies." '

'Oh!' sighed Agatha, 'how I'd love to have red slippers.'

Mother laughed again. 'Don't you see the point? My little goose!'

'Yes,' said Agatha grudgingly, 'I suppose so. But it's not like us. We don't have servants, we are servants. We have to do all the work ourselves. Look at my hands!' She held her chapped hands up despairingly.

'You'll survive,' said Mother. 'We don't have any help because your father doesn't trust . . . doesn't trust anybody else to be here. He thinks harm might come to us if there were others in the house with him so far away.'

'What sort of harm?' I said. 'Murder?'

'No,' Mother smiled at me, 'not that sort of harm. More, a bad influence, manners and morals and that sort of thing.'

'But you're here! Bad influences couldn't happen to us with you here. You teach us to do things right.'

'But . . . oh it doesn't matter.' Mother had given up trying to explain. She sat down, as if she was suddenly exhausted.

'So have we got gentility or not?' I asked.

'Yes, I think we have.'

'And the Howgegos?'

'Oh yes, they've got it, a natural gentility.'

'But Father hasn't?'

'Of course he has!'

'Stupid,' added Agatha, turning her nose up at me, looking adoringly at Mother.

'But you said . . . you said he didn't understand . . .'

'Come on,' said Mother, 'enough of this, you two girls get some potatoes peeled while I see to the twins.'

I scraped my finger in the cold muddy potato water. Why did Agatha always understand better than me? Why would Mother never answer me properly? I could hear her singing to and soothing the babies. I was neither one thing nor the other. I wasn't tall and beautiful and special like Agatha and I wasn't small and weak and needy like the babies. The only person who specially liked me was Isaac, who had a natural gentility, who was the son of a saint. That would have to do.

Ellen and Esther learned to smile and gurgle. They grew fat and rosy, sweet and wholesome as Mrs Howgego's currant buns, and we started to love them. On warm afternoons Aggie and I took them for walks, taking turns to push the pram, leaving Mother in peace. They giggled as the pram bumped and jolted over ruts in the road, and we picked them flowers and leaves to look at and chew. Sometimes we walked all the way to the dyke and the babies eventually slumbered in the pram; and sometimes we called in to see the Howgegos and refreshed ourselves with tea or ginger beer and Mrs Howgego's conversation before we set off home. Often, if Isaac was there and not out rook scaring or stone picking, he would walk some of the way back with us, or with me, for on these occasions, Agatha, thinking herself above us, would walk on ahead with the pram, leaving us to dawdle behind.

On lovely days we stayed away as long as we could, but we always grew nervous as we approached the house. We never quite knew what we would find. On the good days, the days when everything was all right, we would see, relieved, from miles away, the flapping of washing on the line, or else the windows would be flung open to air the house, a beaten rug hanging over a chair outside the door. Or there might be the smells of baking drifting out and even, sometimes, the sound of Mother singing. But there were bad days too when we got home to find Mother drooping in a chair, just as if she had not moved since we had left her. Then she'd start when we opened the door and look at us dully, as if she'd forgotten all about us. On those days we had to ignore our tired feet and our dry throats and make the tea ourselves while Mother struggled wearily to change the twins and hold them to her skinny breasts.

In spring, the pond in the orchard is full of tadpoles which by July have developed into tiny frogs, amazingly delicate detailed perfect frogs, dainty as if they've been fashioned by a jeweller. The cats stalk and pounce upon them, crunch them with their pointed teeth – but there are always plenty more – frogs and toads too.

I used to love catching one, holding it in the prison of my cupped hands and feeling the tiny cold strength of its fury as it leapt and leapt against my fingers to be free; and then suddenly I'd open my hands and it would spring out, high in the air, and plop like a pebble into the pond.

Isaac and I used to spend long afternoons crouched by the water, lifting stones and searching in the long grass for them. If you crept towards the pond from the house and then suddenly stamped your foot they would shoot into the air, twenty or thirty of them at once, and hurl themselves back to the safety of the pond, disappearing with a bubbling plopping beneath the water. After that you had to search for them. There are newts too, that Isaac used to tease with the stems of reeds, chasing them this way and that. There are water boatmen that dimple the skin of the water with their minute weight, and maiden flies, and sometimes, even, a dragonfly that hovers above like royalty, in a shimmer of blue.

It was when Mrs Howgego was with Mother in the house that Isaac and I would wander round the back, would climb the trees, or play round the pond. It is one of those days I remember. The last of them.

It was hot and the twins were sitting up in their pram outside the door, and Davey and Bobby were playing around and Aggie was watching them. Mrs Howgego and Mother were drinking tea in the kitchen, and Isaac and I went round the back to the orchard. We threw a few stones at the barn target, but it was too hot, so we went to play by the pond. We had surprised the froglets already that morning and were searching amongst the grass when Isaac said, 'I reckon there's some really big uns in there, down at the bottom.' We gazed at the muddy inscrutable centre of the pond. 'Shall we go in and catch one?' he said. He looked at me in that awful way he had, his blue eyes gleaming, daring me. I hesitated. I had no wish to go in there. It was a busy pond, oozing and teeming with life, and I did not want to go into it, but I did not want to say no to Isaac either. I wasn't having him calling me a coward.

'Come on Milly,' he said. 'I reckon there could be anything in there. Perhaps even treasure that someone chucked in there hundreds of years ago. There might even be jewels.'

I looked sceptically at the muddy unpromising water, but Isaac had already rolled up his trouser legs and was in up to his ankles.

'That's quite warm,' he said.

'But I'll get my dress filthy!'

'That'll wash. You can tuck it in your drawers, anyway.'

I knew that I had no real choice. Best to get it over with. I tucked up my skirt and stepped tentatively into the water. The bottom of the pond was soft and yielding, the silky mud that squeezed between my toes was oddly warm, like something living.

'See,' said Isaac, 'that's all right.'

It felt as if there were things moving, churning and winding about my ankles. Some slimy green weed clung to my shin. 'Yes,' I said, 'it's all right.'

'Shall we go in the middle then, where it's deeper?'

'I don't mind.'

'I reckon that's where the big uns are,' Isaac said, stepping forward. 'Come on.' He grabbed my hand.

I felt as if I would slip. 'No, don't pull, there's no need to pull,' I said, but he held on to my hand all the same.

'You don't want to go falling down,' he said. 'You just tell me if one of them big uns bites you and I'll get it.'

'Don't,' I shivered. 'Anyway, they don't have teeth, do they? Frogs? I'm sure they don't.'

'Oh yes they do,' said Isaac, 'of course they do. How do you think they eat all them slugs and snails and worms . . . and toes.'

'Why do you always tease me?' I said. 'Anyway, you can't scare me. It's only water. I've never heard of anyone being bitten by a frog!'

Isaac stepped forward again and sank about a foot deeper so that the water came above his knees. 'That's colder here,' he said.

'Let's go,' I said, snatching my hand from his. He tried to grab me again. 'What's the matter? Are you frightened now?' I said, making my voice teasing as his had been.

'I'm sinking!' he said, his eyes wide. 'Quick Milly! Hang on!' and he did indeed seem to be sinking and I reached out my hand and grabbed his again, panicking. I thought I should call Mother, I opened my mouth to call her, but then I saw that he was laughing.

'You'd believe anything. You're daft you are!' he stood up straight. 'Come on, that's quite safe. That's harder on the bottom here.' I swallowed my crossness, and let him tug me deeper in, knowing the only way to get this over was to get on with it.

The water reached half-way up my thighs and just lapped the bottom of my bunched skirts. The bottom of the pond was firmer, though there were things, hard things and sharp things – and worst of all – soft things, that gave under my feet.

We stopped. 'Now what?' I asked. I could not see how we could get the things, the frogs or anything else, without bending down, and we couldn't do that without getting our sleeves wet. Isaac stood looking uncertain for a minute. Then suddenly he splashed his way out.

'I'll have to get my things off,' he said, pulling off his shirt.

'You can't do that!' I gasped.

'Oh can't I?' he said. He hitched his trouser legs up tighter round his thighs and waded back in. He caught my hand again. His chest was very thin and white, I could see all his ribs and his veins under his almost transparent skin. He grinned and began to say something when suddenly Aggie came hurrying round from the front of the house. 'Quick, get out of there! Father's home!'

'Father?' I said. It was so unlikely that he would arrive at this time of day that it took a moment to register.

'Get out of there quickly!' Aggie said urgently, 'and you,' she looked at Isaac, 'better get out of sight.'

But it was too late. Father had followed Agatha round the side of the house. He'd seen me with my skirt all tucked up to show my legs. He'd seen Isaac with half his clothes off holding my hand. I was so shocked I could not even let him go. I just stood dumbly clasping Isaac's hand until he wrenched it away himself. Father didn't speak. He didn't have to. Agatha slunk past him back to the house, and after throwing me a blackly threatening look, Father turned on his heel and followed. Isaac leapt out of the water and struggled into his shirt.

From the house we could hear an explosion of voices. Isaac stood looking at me helplessly. 'I'll have to go,' he said. His face had turned very white so that his freckles stood out darkly.

'Let me come . . . you can't leave me,' I wailed. I grabbed his arm, knowing this was absurd, but I just wanted to hang onto him then, just hang on and run away with my eyes screwed up tight, just run away and never come back.

'Don't be so daft,' said Isaac. 'You don't want any more trouble do you? I'm getting out of here.' He pulled his arm away from me. 'That'll be all right. Don't fret,' he said. He patted me awkwardly on the shoulder. 'See you soon,' he said, and darted off, off like a frightened rabbit round the front of the house, and safely away.

I untucked my skirts and rubbed them over my wet itchy legs. I stood looking at the place where Isaac had been a moment before, and then I felt a cold weight on my leg. I forced myself to look, and then I screamed. I screamed and screamed although the sound would not come at first. There was a thing on my thigh, a huge grey green thing shiny and speckled. I could not move. I did not dare move my leg. I just stood and I screamed and I screamed. I wanted Isaac to come back, but it was Mother who appeared first. The thing was just hanging on my leg, pulsing and swelling.

Mother saw at once what the matter was, and scooped me up in her arms. 'It's all right,' she said softly, 'it's just a leech. We'll soon get it off you.'

Agatha followed behind saying, 'I know what to do. I'll do it shall I? I know what to do. I'll get it off,' dancing around us.

Mother sat me on the kitchen table. 'Will you get out of the way, Agatha!' she snapped, for Agatha was all over the place in her excitement. Mother shoved the poker in the stove, and I started to cry.

'It's all right,' said Agatha, 'it won't burn you. You just have to touch the leech with it and it lets go. You can't cut it off or it leaves its suckers in you!'

'Will you be quiet, Agatha!' said Mother, for this information only made me cry louder, but even in my terrified condition I registered this scolding of Agatha on my behalf, and saved it up to remember.

Father stood looking grimly down during this performance, and Mrs Howgego looked at me kindly but dared not speak.

'Don't cry, Milly pet,' said Mother. 'Just hold still.' She took the glowing poker from the fire and then I shut my eyes as she touched the leech which let go at once and fell onto the floor, a shrivelling blood-gorged lump.

There was a momentary pause, everyone looking at the dying leech which leaked my blood onto the clean floor; and then I began to shudder and sob again; and Mother to comfort, and the twins to bawl, and Father to shout at Mrs Howgego.

'Get out of my house!' he shouted. I saw his face flash red and there were bubbles of spit on his lips. 'Get out of here, you whore. And keep your filthy urchins away from my daughters!'

I looked helplessly at Mrs Howgego and I saw that her lovely face had changed. Her smiling mouth had shrunk to a mean and tatty buttonhole. Her eyes were chips of ice. She picked up her basket. 'Goodbye Phyllida,' she said. 'Goodbye Agatha and Milly.' I could see her natural gentility then, I could see it in the way she looked so dignified beside our flushed and furious father, as she turned and lifted Davey onto her hip and grabbed the hand of wide-eyed Bobby, and swept them away.

It was ages before I saw Isaac again. That day hurt Mother. It sent her tumbling downwards in a sad and silent spiral. There were no more songs or rhymes. She did not want to speak of that day. She would not answer my questions. I did not understand. Father had forbidden that whore, Mrs Howgego, to visit: Mother pined for Mrs Howgego, the saint. She would not explain. Her face grew pinched, and streaks of grey appeared quite suddenly in the dark of her hair. Her little thought frown became permanent and other lines creased her face.

Father told Mother never to let the girls near those scabby beggars again; never to let that slut, me, out of the house.

'But she's only ten, Charles! She's a child!'

'She knows what's what. You can see it in her eyes. Any daughter of yours . . .'

No. I did not understand. I knew I had done something bad. It was awful, it was to do with Isaac. But nothing I had done was that bad, was it? There was all that muddiness and slime and wet.

There was Isaac's frail skin with the blue veins showing through. And there was the leech. I was a little slut and not to be trusted, that's all I understood. Though what a slut was, I was not certain.

Mother crumpled when he said words like that, like slut and whore and bastard, she sagged with a weight I did not understand. All I did understand was that I had done something terrible and that I had made things worse for my mother. I had heard her say, once, 'I don't know what I'd do without you, Candida,' but now there was no more Mrs Howgego. Mother had lost the will to disobey. She lost her will to do anything much. She became so quiet that it was a surprise to hear her voice. She even let herself get dirty, neglected her hair so that it grew wild and tangled. She lost her clean soapy smell. Was stale.

Agatha and I were quiet too. We were frightened but we could not speak to Mother. It was hard even to speak to each other. Too frightening, for what could we do? We simply got on with it. We looked after the twins almost entirely. Mother would not feed them any more and they were soon weaned, seemed grateful to forget her thin grey milk, and thrived and grew happier and fatter. They were soon creeping about in need of constant watchfulness. Mother hardly looked at them, except to grab and hug them fiercely now and then, tears standing in her eyes. Agatha and I did almost everything: the cleaning, the washing, the cooking. We were only little girls, but we learned to do it all. Agatha milked the cow and fed the hens and cleared the garden. How did Agatha know just what to do? I've never understood that. How did she know what to do about the leech? And you'd never guess, now, to look at her, useless article that she is.

Father stopped coming home. What was there to come home for? Though we tried, Aggie and I, the house was never as much a home as it had been before the time when Ellenanesther were born. That was when it all went wrong. It all went wrong. And Mother died in late October when the sky was dark by tea-time; when it had been raining for a week; when the house was cold and grimy; when Father hadn't been home for almost a month.

She simply went out and never came back. She kissed us before she left. She said she loved us, and that we must forgive her. She said we must try and understand. And then she went out into the dark and the rain, and she never returned.

Aggie and I sat up all that night waiting for her to come back. We kept the fire burning, and a kettle of water on the stove ready to make her tea, ready for her to wash herself with. We put her slippers on the hearth to warm, but I didn't really think we would ever see her again. It was as if she had been leaving us for a long time, becoming thinner and paler and further away.

I have a dream that I am Mother sometimes on the worst nights of all. It is a dream I struggle to wake from. It is worse than the dreams about Father. The rain is cold and merciless in my dream, it pelts needle-sharp into my face. My coat is soaked, my hat, my lovely London hat disintegrates and a paper pansy falls off and catches in the crook of my elbow before falling into the mud. I just wish I could be in London, I wish fiercely that I could be there in all the noise and warmth, the bustle and friendliness of it, for here there is nothing. Only unfriendly darkness, a flat and empty nothing, only rain, only cold. I rush forward through a streaming void. Oh that would be the thing! To run there, to run away, to run and run and leave this cold bleak nothing of a place and find a way back. I can sing. I can sing. I *can*. I could find my way back. I could. Oh yes I could. But behind me there is that other thing. Behind me is a house full of draughts, full of mouths I should be feeding, mouths I should be causing to smile. That house is a big draughty box packed with guilt. Oh I love them but I cannot be doing with it any more, any of it. I cannot. When those twins were born I started to die and I've been dying from the outside inwards ever since. And now there's just a tiny streak, just a sliver, a living core inside this cold body. I cannot go on. There is so little of me left, such a meagre shred of me inside this cold woman's body.

Sometimes the wind that blows for miles, that blows round and through the house, through the doors and windows, blows through me too. Inside I billow and bloat, there is a great empty space, like the inside of a church and in the centre there is a candle. One small lighted candle, its flame flapping feebly in the wind. It has stayed alight so far, that little flame, but it cannot for ever. And now the wind drives needles of rain into my face, into my eyes.

I am so cold, so small and cold – and here is the dyke. It is a seam of deepness that threads the shallow muddiness of it all. Blacker than the ground, than the sky; richer than the air that carries such a thin slanting of rain, such a meagre spiteful wetness.

My feet have carried me here and now they have gone. There is a numbness beyond coldness. My feet have disappeared and my hands, and my cheeks too have numbed away, and my lips, and my hair is thick and wet and heavy as weed. Frozen. I never want to thaw. I could not bear the pain of it. I am here. I am beside the black rush of water, carried here by feet I no longer own. The wind is roaring, a base beast, a greedy monotonous beast that spits in my eyes. The water is the place. The dyke. The water is the only place to get away, to fill my ears, to stop the sound, the roaring and the pricking, to wash away the rest of the feeling.

And then I have to wake. I have to wake or else the water the taste of water fills my mouth and I have to fight, to struggle up out of it, out of the cruel drowning flood of dream.

And it is only a dream. I am not Mother. I do not know. It is only that someone saw her stumbling forward one terrible night. He shouted but she did not hear. It was only that they found the pansy from her hat, from her lovely hat, all wet and muddy near the edge.

*   *   *

Sometimes, in the night, Agatha sleepwalks. There is something in the sound of her footfalls, a sort of smoothness unlike her normal stiff gait, that tells me she is asleep. Sometimes it is only in her room that she walks. There is a gliding, light and ghost-like, and then the creak as she returns to bed.

But sometimes she comes down the stairs, past my door, past Ellenanesther's doors and down to the kitchen. I don't know what she does in the kitchen. I do not follow. I am frightened of a sleeping woman walking about in the house, a sleeping woman with God knows what going on behind her blank eyes. This house is a mad house, with Agatha fast asleep, but pacing, pacing; with Ellenanesther's muttering vibrating through the walls; with that moaning from the cellar. Only some nights this happens. At other times it is quiet, and whether we sleep or no there is an air of restfulness in the house. But tonight . . . tonight Aggie *is* moving up there, but not sleepwalking. She is moving the furniture. Yes she is! The bitch. There she goes . . . a heavy thing – her bed? Where she gets the strength from I don't know. *One of these days you'll come through the floor, Agatha.* No, the house will not stand much more of it. Surely, the house cannot stand it, this constant movement. The crack in my ceiling is longer, surely it is, is wider. Can Aggie never be still?

Tonight my mind is restless too. I do not think that I will sleep tonight. I dare not sleep. There is the constant thrumming of the rain and the other noises of the night. The sounds of the cats hunting and the occasional scream of their victims; the wet squeaky scritch-scratching of branches on the windows; Agatha moving about; Ellenanesther muttering; George groaning. This house is like the inside of my skull, tumbled and unstill, unrested. The worst things will not rest tonight. Will not.

*   *   *

I have a good memory, a sight better than Agatha's, but I cannot recall clearly the days that followed the night that Mother went away. Father came back and was grim, and did not talk to us. We had to listen at doors and we pieced together the bits. Someone brought Father a damp and muddy scrap, a purple paper scrap of pansy from her lovely hat. Someone saw her rushing forward, and they shouted but she did not hear.

Mrs Howgego came but Father would not let her near. She stood outside and there were tears in her eyes, and Isaac was with

73

her and his hair was combed and he was looking down and kicking at the dirt, embarrassed, but Father would not let them in. She went away at last and she took with her the heavy basket full of things she'd brought for us. Isaac looked back and I think he saw my face at the upstairs window. I think he must have done, and I think he smiled. I wanted to open the window and jump out and go home with them, and live with them and be a Howgego. But I did not. I just sat there in my mourning dress and watched them grow tiny, watched them disappear.

After Mother, there was the time when we still went to church with Father, the time when he would rub our heads before he went away: 'Stay away from the dyke,' he'd say. How long that time lasted I am uncertain. It was a long time, long enough for Agatha to grow into a young woman who preened in front of an old mirror, who dreamed of being adored, but was too haughty even to look at any of the young men in the congregation. It was long enough for Ellenanesther to grow from fat babies into strange pretty girls for whom nothing much existed except each other. It was years. They were uneasy and strange years. Father was seldom at home and we were very much alone. After that time when he would not let her in, Mrs Howgego did not come back. I wished and wished that she would, and that Isaac would, just turn up one day, but I did not dare go to them and then the longer it was, the longer the time went on, the more impossible it seemed. Sometimes I caught a glimpse of a boy that might have been Isaac, nearby, a flicker of a boy that might have been only one of my own wishes, or might have been Isaac, but I could never be sure.

It was years. That time went on for years. There was nothing we wanted for, but company. We had clothes and food, and Father brought books for us, instructive books, that told us to count our blessings and honour our father and keep ourselves clean and ladylike.

After the time of Aggie's curse, there was Isaac again for me, of course, and Mrs Howgego began to call again. And there were other people sometimes, of course there were. There was Sara Gotobed who brought the groceries when Father was so seldom home. Once or twice people called, lost people, or people walking about looking for work who found our house and knocked, and we would sometimes open the door, and sometimes not. For Father frightened us. He told us such things about other people, town people, and how they were such thieves and cheats, and how they preyed on girls alone, and terrible stories, so that although we longed for company we were afraid of it too.

And there was the summer when our second cousin came to call. Father had no family, he said, but Mother said it was not that. He had family but he had estranged himself she said, and he would not talk of it. But our second cousin came to call, with his friend. It was a summer evening and the sky was aswoop with swallows and there were bats, and one almost tangled in my hair . . . and the friend held my arm, Roger his name was, he held my arm with his strong soldier's hand, his hand that had held a gun brushed against the side of my breast. And it was my knee he touched inside my skirt. Not Agatha's.

I should have married Isaac. I would have been Mrs Howgego, old Mrs Howgego now, and my grandchildren would come to call. I blame Agatha. No. Father was to blame . . . but still I feel angry with Agatha.

It was the war that changed things, set everything askew. Here there was little sign of it. It had nothing to do with us, so far away. We read about it in Father's newspapers when he came home, and of course Isaac was full of it. He couldn't wait to get away and be a part of it. To be a hero. But Mr Howgego died just before the outbreak of war, and Ben and Abel went to France, so Isaac had to stay at home and help provide for his mother and the youngsters.

He grew up in those years, oh yes he did. I did too, of course. I started my bleeding, my curse, and it was not such a drama as Aggie's had been. How Aggie loves a drama! All her life what she's really lacked has been an audience. My grown-upness was not such a shock. It was not such a serious thing as Aggie's had seemed. I felt no different. I was still a girl, still the same Milly, still enjoyed doing the same things. Once it had started I went outside and tried them all: I climbed trees, and hunted frogs and threw apples at the barn and it felt just the same to me. There was nothing magical. I didn't feel closer to Agatha or Mrs Howgego. It was just another chore to deal with. The grown-upness did come, but gradually. It was not to do with the bleeding, or with the stealthy swelling of my breasts. It was to do with worry and longing and nostalgia and hope; and to do with the change of my feelings towards Isaac. And, though I say I'm grown-up, there is still a part of this old woman that is nine years old, that still hears with terror Mother's cries on the afternoon of Ellenanesther's birth. There is still part of me that longs to bury my face in my mother's hair and feel her hold me tight, make everything all right.

Mrs Howgego used to watch us, Isaac and me, after that time. I told her, of course, and she offered the same advice to me as to Agatha. I must keep myself nice and then no babies would come. She tried to keep Isaac away from me, or at least away from me when she wasn't there to keep an eye on us.

Isaac managed to overhear the conversation I had with Mrs Howgego about it all. 'What do that feel like?' he asked.

'Nothing much,' I said.

'So you're a woman now?' he looked me up and down. 'You still don't look it.'

'I'm not a woman, stupid,' I said, 'so you can stop staring at me. And I'm not going to stop playing with you just because of some stupid curse.'

He looked relieved. 'But Mam says we shouldn't be alone together. She reckons that's not right.'

It was not then that it made any difference, but the years passed by, a long procession of green and gold and red and grey; wind and rain and sun and storm. Father came and went away. We were forever anxiously awaiting his arrival, for although it was seldom, it could be at any time. He might arrive at midnight or first light or mid-afternoon. He might not come for two months and then he might return within a day or two, or change his mind and turn back an hour or so after he left. Once he was with us we were always tense, awaiting his departure, holding our breath and crossing our fingers behind our backs that he would leave before he found something to anger him. And when the Howgegos were with us we were nervous. What if Father returned suddenly and found them there? And if we were out walking, especially if we visited the Howgegos, we were afraid on the way home that he would be there waiting. He was hardly with us and yet he was with us all the time. There was no freedom from him. I used to watch from my window sometimes, for his shape appearing in the distance growing larger, growing into Father, and I was pleased when I saw him for at least it was novelty. At least I did not have to strain my ears and eyes for him. I had only to guard my tongue.

The different feelings grew between Isaac and me over the years. I loved Isaac like a brother for a long time, I wished he was my brother – and then I was glad he was not. I remember a day when Mrs Howgego was in our kitchen, and Isaac and I were standing outside and we were talking. He was a good deal taller than me and I tilted my face up to his. The gold of an early sunset glinted on the wetness all around us and as he looked down at me the light caught the ends of his long lashes and made his eyes shine a darker blue and I found myself aching for him. He was so beautiful and young and yet a man. There was the softness of a young moustache on his lip, tender blonde and soft, and it was no sisterly love I felt for him then. I knew his mother's eyes were upon us. We were not touching, but I was aware that the air that was touching me was touching him too. I could feel Mrs Howgego looking at us, thinking she could stop it, and I felt a realization of my power over Isaac. Oh yes, it had been the other way round when we were children. Then he was the brave one, the tease, but I could see that he was looking at me differently now. He was puzzled and looked afraid of what he was feeling.

'Mam's watching,' he murmured.

'So,' I said. 'We're not doing anything wrong.'

'No,' he agreed uncertainly.

'But I would like,' I murmured, 'not to be nice any more, Isaac.'

He breathed sharply in, but his eyes never left mine.

At that moment, Mrs Howgego chose to come abruptly out of the house. She had not heard what I'd said, I'm sure, but she looked at me oddly. She must have felt the way the air was almost crackling between us, and sensed danger.

'Come on Isaac,' she said. 'We'd better get along back now and see what Bobby and Davey are up to.'

I shook my head at him. He looked from one of us to the other but his eyes rested with me. 'You go on, Mam,' he said. 'I'll catch you up.'

'Won't you walk along with me?' she said.

'I won't be long,' he repeated, hardly glancing in her direction.

She stood for a moment, indecisively, and then she sighed. 'Well mind that you come along in a minute then,' she said. 'You don't let him hang around, Milly, do you hear?' I nodded. 'What your poor mam would do now I don't hardly like to think. Don't you be long now,' she added again, and giving me a very dubious look, left us.

I waited until she was a good way off and then I reached out my hands and held his. It was the first loving gesture. We had held hands often enough as children, carelessly, as a convenience or as part of a game, but now, suddenly, the feel of him was precious.

'I can't do that to you, Milly,' he said. 'That's not right.'

'But we could get married,' I said. 'We could, and then it would be right. It would be *nice*.'

'Are you off your rocker?' he asked. 'Your dad'd kill us! and I don't reckon my mam'd like it either.'

78

'Don't you want to marry me?' I asked.

'Of course I do,' he said and he squeezed my hands. 'Oh Milly . . . but not yet. I can't keep a wife yet. And then there's the war . . .'

'But you're not going.'

'Don't be so sure.'

'You can't go, Isaac,' I said. 'What would I do?'

'What do you ever do?'

We fell silent. It hurt that he said that though I knew it was not in Isaac to be deliberately cruel. But he was quite right. What did I ever do, but wait and hope? 'I can't just stay here like this,' I said. 'It's awful, Isaac. It never changes. The four of us in the house. We don't even know what day it is sometimes. Do you understand that? And always there's the fear that Father could arrive. Always, we are bored or we are scared. Always. It is so awful Isaac. It's like a prison. It feels just like a prison.'

'Don't be so daft, girl,' said Isaac, but he put his arms around me. 'Look at the sky! You can see forever. That's no prison.'

I pressed myself against him, smelling his warm gingery smell, feeling the warmth of his body, the thin strength of his arms holding me tight. I clenched my eyes against the tears that threatened. It felt so safe, to be held like this. I felt safer than I'd felt since Mother. 'But you mustn't leave me,' I whispered. 'You must promise you will never leave me.'

Isaac's arms loosened and he held me away from him. 'I can't promise that,' he said. 'But if I did go away I'd come back for you.'

'No you wouldn't!' I said, and the tears burst from my eyes. I buried my head against him again. 'Why would you want to come back once you'd got away from here?'

'For you,' he said. His arms held me so strongly. 'I'd come back for you.' I let him hold me. It was good to be held so close to him, to another body, but there was no real comfort in it. He didn't know. Sometimes lately, compared to myself, Isaac seemed a great big simple boy. He didn't understand, as I did, about all the things there are in the world, all the people. There are restaurants where women dine with men who are not their husbands and where ice swans melt in pools of crystal light. In London there is bustle and brightness and sparkle. There is music and the streets are full of laughter. That is the world that Mother remembered.

'How do you know?' I mumbled. 'How do you know that you wouldn't meet someone else?'

'I would come back,' said Isaac stubbornly. 'I've been away before and come back. I've been nearly to Cambridge. Anyway, I reckon I'd better go now. Mam will be looking for me.'

I pulled away. 'Oh go then. Run after your mam.'

'Don't be like that,' said Isaac. 'You know I've got to go.'

'Oh Isaac,' I said, grasping his sleeve again. 'Why don't we both go?'

'What are you on about now?'

'Both go away from here. Run away together, to London perhaps. We could get married there. There is plenty of work. There are factories. We could rent a house. Just you and me, Isaac! Can you imagine it? A little house in a busy street, all noise and bustle! Every night I'd cook our tea and then we could walk the streets. I'd hold your arm and we could walk along and look at all the people. We could go to the music-hall. I so want to go and see what it was like for Mother. And then we would have a baby of our own, a sweet girl, or maybe a lovely bonny boy, a Howgego boy, and then we'd be a proper family.'

'You're daft,' said Isaac, shaking his head. Oh he did make me angry sometimes!

'Why?' I demanded.

'How could we? I couldn't leave Mam. Your dad'd murder us.'

'But he'd never find us.'

He hugged me again. 'Oh Milly.'

'Isaac,' I said urgently, 'I told you, I cannot stay here. Something will happen to me if I stay here much longer. I just don't think I can stand it.'

The coldness of a sudden shower of rain surprised us. It had been alternately wet and dry all day and now the sky was darkening quickly.

'I'll have to go,' said Isaac.

'No,' I said, 'don't go yet. It won't last long. Come into the barn with me. I don't want to go inside yet.'

'But Mam . . .'

'Just five minutes more.'

He followed me into the gloomy barn. There was an old bench by the wall in the darkest corner near the cow's stall. I brushed some straw off it. 'Sit down with me,' I said. We sat down. I felt awkward. It was as if, suddenly, we were strangers. The air smelt sweetly of rain and hay and cow. The rain pattered on the roof, coming through at one end where there was a hole. It was quite dark in the barn and cosy with the sound of the cow chewing the cud.

Isaac put his arm round my shoulder and kissed me. It was a long deep kiss. We both pulled away after a moment, trembling with what it made us feel. I tried to pull him back to me, I put my hand behind his head. I wanted more kisses. It was so delicious, the feel of his mouth, the taste of his mouth. It was like drinking when you are thirsty, impossible not to go on and on. He held back for a moment. 'I won't be able to stop . . .' he murmured, but I was kissing him again and feeling him trembling, and I did not want to stop.

'I love you Isaac,' I said, and I held him tight against me and I knew it was the animal thing that I wanted; the thing that Isaac had told me; the thing the bull had done to Barley. It didn't seem so awful now. I understood now. There was a place inside me, a space that ached for him. I just wanted him completely to be mine. And if there was a child because of it, then we would be married and then he would never leave me, then I would escape and bring an end to this terrible time, this terrible empty trap of a time that was my life. It seemed so simple suddenly.

But Isaac pulled away again. 'No,' he said, and he was breathing hard. 'Stop that, Milly.'

'Are you scared?' I teased, and I ran my hand along his thigh. He shuddered. 'When we're married,' he said. 'I want you Milly, but when we're married.'

'I want you now,' I said. My belly felt as if it was dissolving. All I wanted was the feel of him, the weight of him against me. 'We will get married so it's not wrong . . . come on Isaac . . .'

He stood up and tried to turn away, but I stood up too and held on to him and he stopped resisting and he pressed himself against me and then we were on the floor in the straw, and his hands fumbled and fought with my dress and his lips closed on my nipple. He was like a baby, a nuzzling whimpering baby, and his hands under my dress found the place. Oh I whimpered too then, and moaned in an animal way that frightened and thrilled me and then I touched him and felt the hot silk of his thing, and I saw the high straining purpleness of it like a terrible flower there in the gloomy barn. And he was mine. Isaac was my lover. I felt his heart beating against me and he filled up the aching space and his tears wet my breast and he moaned and shuddered. And then he lay still.

'Are you all right?' he said after a moment, leaning up on one elbow.

I did not feel all right. It was lovely. It had been lovely but I was not ready to stop. 'Is that it?' I said.

'What are you on about?' he said. 'Of course that's it!' He stood up and fastened his belt. 'I'll have to get off now.' He leant down and kissed me, and picked some bits of straw out of my hair. 'I love you too,' he said awkwardly. 'You get yourself in the house now.'

He kissed me again, chastely on the head, and then he left me. I listened to him hurry away and then I sat where I was until it was dark and I heard Agatha's worried voice calling me. I ran over and over it all in my mind, wondering why it was that I felt so disappointed. I had had what I wanted and it had not hurt at all, it was not horrible at all, it was just a disappointment. Perhaps it was better between people who were properly married? But as I stood up and brushed myself down I smiled. Not nice. I'm not nice now I thought, with satisfaction.

Perhaps it was wrong, the way I led Isaac on. Led him on! As if he was some dull mindless beast, that needs a halter or a ring through the nose, that needs a prod with a stick. No, he was no animal. He was a man with a brain, with a will of his own. He knew what would happen if he followed me into the barn. He didn't have to follow. I was desperate to escape and it was the only thing I could think of. The only way out. Although as it turned out, it wasn't. And we did it again and again, and I really loved Isaac. We were never married in a church, but no married people could have felt closer, adored and worshipped each other more. My body cried out for his when he was away.

*   *   *

Late at night, in the aloneness of the night, when the house creaks and the branches scrape and tap, when bleached moonlight spills dustily through my ragged curtains; or nights like tonight when the rain streams from the sky in a river of black silk, my body still cries out for his. Oh yes, I am an old woman and my breasts are long and withered and whiskery as rats. I am old and broad and the skin on my body is crumpled and the hair on my head and my body is sparse and grey, and the veins writhe and knot on my thighs like eels. All this is true but there is still a part of me that cries out for Isaac. I lie. It need not be Isaac. It cries out for a man. Oh yes! That part of me is alive and ticking.

Agatha is crashing about now. It sounds as if she is hurling things at the walls. Perhaps she too is frustrated. Perhaps her old body wants it too. *Is that it, Agatha? You need a good fuck.* Shout what you like, she'll not hear above her constant movement. One day she'll come through the ceiling and break in a splinter of old furniture, old sticks of old furniture and old brittle bones.

Tomorrow, when Mark comes with the groceries, with the gin and the olives and the biscuits and the cat-food and the modern Chinese food that only needs a stir, I will bring him in. A nice presentable boy he is. He makes an effort to be friendly, stops for a few words. He has manners, nice ways, and he has time for a house full of mad old women. I will lure him into the house. What can I say? 'There's something I want to show you upstairs. Please, Mark . . .' I don't think he'd refuse if I asked very nicely. He's too well brought up. He couldn't refuse without seeming rude. And once I had him in here, what couldn't I do with him! He's about as tall as Isaac, but he's dark – Agatha likes them dark – black hair, a spindly moustache. His face is a bit spotty, but that is only youth. He wears very tight trousers and there is a bulge quite plainly visible. He's quite shameless in those tight trousers, little bottom, skinny legs – but strong, and that bulge. Sometimes I don't know where to look! What does he think we think, flaunting like that the secret part of him, bunched up like that under that stretched material?

I could undress him. If he tried to resist I could tie him up. Oh how could I? He's so young and strong. The muscles stand out on his arms when he carries the heavy box of food. Never mind that now. I would manage. I would tie him to my bed, hands on the rails at the top and I would peel off those tight trousers and he would be mine. How that bulge would spring up with the freedom I would give it! And he would be mine. I could sit upon him and ride him, up and down, and fill myself with him so young and strong, fill myself to my heart's content. I could keep him a prisoner, feed him up, wash him, and use him whenever I wanted. He would be surprised at this old woman.

Imagine what Aggie would say if I had Mark like that! She's only had it in the most wicked of ways. She doesn't know how it feels to do it out of love and adoration, to be filled with desire and then to have that desire satisfied by a strong young man. The nearest she got was spying on me when I walked out with Roger and he touched my breast and his hand touched my knee inside my skirt. She coveted my experience, she converted my experience into her own. Oh how she steals my memories! She hates me because I've had more success with men. I was the most attractive to men. She was supposed to be so beautiful with her slender body and the haughty way she held her head – and look where it got her!

Scraggy Aggie, up there in the attic using your energy to demolish the house. What do you think will come of it? If there was a way to make it right, to arrange it so that it was all right, so that you felt comfortable, you would have found it long ago. But if you did? If, magically, it all fell into place . . . Ah yes! Of course! The bed *here* not there; and the dressing-table like so. And then the chair beside it . . . perfect! What then Agatha? Would you then be still?

* * *

Isaac and I lay in Mrs Howgego's bed. She had gone to the village and Isaac was supposed to be watching his younger brothers. Isaac dozed, and I turned away from him and nuzzled my face into the rumpled sheets that smelled faintly of Mrs Howgego. It felt wrong doing it in here, in a way it did not in the barn or under the trees by the dyke. Mrs Howgego's things were all around. Her old bulky bunion-shaped everyday shoes were planted squarely on the floor, and I could almost see her in them, hands on hips, expression of disgust and disappointment on her face. Her private things, underclothes and her nightdress, were draped on the chair by the bed. I did not want to look. In the passion of lovemaking I had not cared where we were, but now it felt awful to be here in Mrs Howgego's bed with Mrs Howgego's son. I shook Isaac's shoulder.

'Wake up. I'm going downstairs.'

'Frightened?' he asked.

'No, it just feels wrong being here.'

'Just lie still a minute, girl,' mumbled Isaac and he snuggled his head down on my shoulder. 'I reckon you're the loveliest . . .'

'Oh stop now, Isaac,' I said and pushed him away. 'Let's get up and go outside. See what the boys are up to.'

He held on to me. 'Wait. I've been thinking. About what you said . . . about us going away together . . .'

'Isaac!'

'Wait. I int sure yet, but, I reckon we should make some sort of plans. I might still go away to war, but I want us to marry, Milly. I love you.'

I wound my arms around him, tight, smelling his familiar skin. I did not know what to say. I just held him tight. I just held on to him. If it would happen, if it would come true, then everything would be all right after all.

He laughed, 'I thought you were getting up?'

'I am,' I said. I could hear Bobby's voice outside, shouting something to Davey. They would be my brothers. Isaac's brothers would be mine too. I hugged him again and then sat up. 'Let's go and make some tea,' I said.

'I reckon you ought to get going,' said Isaac, 'before Mam comes back. And there's your . . .'

'He won't be back today,' I said.

'You don't know that.'

'No, but . . .' I did not want to spoil it all by thinking of Father. He would kill me, and Isaac, if he could see us now. I tried to block him from my mind when we were together, but always he was there. Always as I looked past Isaac's shoulder the fear of seeing him was there. Quickly I stood up and began pulling on my clothes.

'You're beautiful,' Isaac said.

'I must go, you're right, I must get back,' I said. It was all right. He had said what I needed him to say. I could go now. I felt that I could go. I could go home and treasure the words he'd spoken, and plan and dream.

He got out of bed too and began dressing. It was different both standing together in a bedroom, dressing, different to fumbling about outside on the ground. This was how it would be when I was Mrs Howgego.

'Do you really think I'm beautiful?' I asked, looking at my flushed face in Mrs Howgego's mirror.

'Yes,' said Isaac. 'Of course I do. I love you.'

'Yes, but . . . am I really beautiful? To other people? Because when I look in the mirror, I see just *me*. It's hard to tell, isn't it? I think I look quite . . . pleasant, quite passable, but I'm a bit small and fat aren't I? And my hair is just brown.' Isaac stood behind me, put his arms around me from behind, so that I could see his face reflected beside mine.

'Well,' he considered. 'I suppose you're not beautiful in the way Aggie is, but . . .'

I stiffened inside his arms. I saw my mirrored face stiffen. 'So you think Agatha is more beautiful than me?' I pulled away and turned to face him.

'Yes, no . . . I mean yes, I reckon she might be to most people who didn't . . . but not to . . . oh I don't know!' he stretched out his arms to me but I moved away. 'Oh don't, Milly. That's not fair. You asked and I told you. It's you I love.'

'You didn't have to say Agatha was more beautiful!' I wailed. 'She's not inside . . . if you knew what she was like.'

'I don't think her more beautiful!'

'You said you did!' I swept out of the room and clattered down the stairs with him following me. I ignored him. I picked up my basket from Mrs Howgego's kitchen and went outside into the brightness. 'Are you all right?' I asked Davey, who was sitting on the step.

'What were you doing in my mam's room?' he asked, sulkily.

'Just talking. Have you been having fun?'

'No. Bobby won't let me go on the swing. Are you going home? Can I walk along with you and Zac?'

'Isaac's not coming,' I said.

'Had a row?' he asked with his head on one side. 'Never mind. That'll soon blow over.' I laughed for he sounded exactly like his mother.

'Not really,' I said. It wasn't Isaac I was angry with, not really; it was Aggie. I waited for a moment hoping that Isaac would come out, but he didn't. I could imagine him skulking in the kitchen. I could have gone back in and said sorry. I should have done. I knew I was being stupid. But I couldn't. I needed time. I had spent my life knowing how superior Aggie was to me, in looks, in height, in the way she could sing and play, in the way she was so like Mother; and hearing Isaac say she was more beautiful really stung. I was only cross with him for not lying. But then he would not have been Isaac if he had.

I went home. I knew he would come soon, perhaps the next day. I was not worried. He had asked me to marry him, that was what mattered. Only when he didn't turn up did I begin to wonder what I'd done. I watched Agatha slyly; tall graceful Agatha working in the garden, sweeping the barn, carrying milk. I watched the clear line of her jaw, and the way her dark lashes cast shadows on the dusky rose of her cheeks. She was beautiful, but not absolutely beautiful. What I liked to look at most was her nose.

I stood by the mirror gazing at my face, my perfectly pleasant face, wavering in the light of a candle. It was my father's face, only softer and rounder. Serious, brown-haired, straight-nosed, round-cheeked. Perfectly good enough for Isaac, lanky freckly Isaac with his floppy hair and his big clumsy hands and feet. Oh so stupid! The thought of Agatha and Isaac together! I was flooded with love for him. In the morning, I vowed, I would go. I would not care what Mrs Howgego thought. I would go to him and tell him I understood, that I loved him, so so much. I even considered setting off then, in the middle of the night. Whatever would Mrs Howgego say to that? She'd been different with me in the months since Isaac and I had become lovers. She was a bit stiff and odd with me, and once or twice I'd caught her staring at me, a speculative look in her eyes. It was almost as if she could see inside me. It made me hot and uncomfortable when she looked at me like that. I am sure that she knew what we did together, that we were, in a natural way, man and wife.

I smiled at myself in the mirror. I looked better when I smiled. Milly Howgego, I mouthed. Then I started, I could hear something outside. Immediately I thought of Isaac, I held my breath, my heart leaping joyfully in my breast – but then I realized it was not Isaac's footsteps I could hear. It was Father's. My rising hope fell like a stone in my belly. Quickly I licked my finger and thumb and nipped the candle flame between them so that it died with a soft hiss, and then I crept up the stairs. Tomorrow was soon enough to see Father.

As soon as I saw Father at breakfast time, I knew something had changed. He was different, more cheerful, no, more *purposeful* than he'd been ever since Mother's passing. The air of nervousness that always hovered over our times with Father dispersed a little – though we were still wary. Father's moods could change as suddenly as a snap of the fingers. Some little thing, a careless word, any evidence of a slip in our manners or politeness, could send him plummeting into a foul mood that bruised and thickened the air in the room and made me feel faint with anxiety.

Once, I forgot myself and rested my elbows on the table for a second, and then when he snapped at me to sit up straight, I apologized with my mouth full. He threw a milk-jug at me for that, and smashed it – Mother's cherished jug that we hardly ever used for fear of breaking it – and then he sent me to my room. I was grateful to be there, out of his way, but I brooded. I spent the day hating him. He did not have natural gentility, whatever Mother had said.

But this time it was different. Father ate a plate full of bacon and eggs and toast, and pushed his cup towards Agatha for some more tea. He took his pipe, with its long curved stem, from his pocket, and he filled it with tobacco and lit it. Then he leant back in his chair, puffing.

'I must say,' he said, as the cool grey smoke floated out of his mouth, 'you've done a quite remarkable job here. You've kept things very nice indeed. I will admit that I pondered on the wisdom of leaving four such youngsters alone out here, but I can see I made the right decision.'

'We've done our best,' said Agatha.

'Yes. I can see that. You're done well, with no help. You do understand, I could not countenance having another person here, another influence. But there's no need for it. You live a simple life here away from corruption. I cannot risk you becoming corrupted. I am right, am I? There is nothing you want for. Is there?'

'No, Father,' we all said, promptly.

'You've been good children bearing up to the terrible loss of your mother so bravely. The time has come to begin to think about the future.'

The future! I did not dare look at him. What future could there be for us but marriage? I forced myself to look down, to be demure, to be silent, although the words bulged in my mouth. Isaac. I would marry Isaac. That would be my future. I would marry Isaac whatever Father said, and then everything would be all right. I would be safe.

'Yes,' he continued. 'You're good girls, good children. I think of you often, and fondly, while I am away. It comforts me to know you are here, tucked away. I grew up in this house, as you know, and my childhood was exemplary. It was not until I was exposed to the world that I even knew that evil existed. People will lie and steal and cheat. Worse things become of women than you could possibly dream. That is why I want to protect you. You are mine and I will keep you pure. I would kill anyone who laid a finger on you, or who spoke an impure word to any one of you. Do you understand?'

'Yes, Father,' we all said. His voice as he had spoken was calm and cool. Cool blue smoke floated around him. His pipe gurgled slightly as he sucked upon it.

He looked from one of us to the other. His eyes passed quickly over Agatha. She did not look like a good child. She looked like a vital young woman, tall and slender with a curving woman's shape. He never looked long at Agatha these days. It was as if he was afraid of what he might see if he let his eyes linger, but she looked at him with her dark dewy eyes.

'Father,' she said, daringly, glancing at me for support. 'There is only one thing that we would like. We were wondering if . . . although the dresses we have are lovely, if we could have something a little more grown-up next time. More like Mother used to . . .' she tailed off. I couldn't look at Father. I was afraid that this would rouse his temper – but no – Agatha was a better judge of his present mood than me. He was secure today, against such trivial knocks. She darted me a look.

'The twins have outgrown their dresses . . . they're shooting up,' I offered diplomatically.

'Ellen and Esther, stand up,' Father said. They did so, their movements synchronized. They were at a gawky stage, had grown several inches in the past few months, and their dresses were indeed too small. 'Mmm,' said Father. 'All right, sit down.'

He frowned at the way they moved together and shook his head. Then he switched his attention back to Aggie and me and began to talk. He talked about the running of the house and the way he had organized things financially so that we would always have enough to live on. All we had to do was carry on in the same way and we would never want for anything, no matter what happened to him. He'd looked around, he said, and found several things that needed attention, gates and windows to be fixed and the house to be repainted outside, for all the old paint was peeling off. As he talked a dreadful feeling grew in me. Perhaps he was planning to come back here and live more with us. The horror with which this idea filled me was mixed with guilt for feeling the horror. After all, this was his home. He was a good man really, wasn't he? Surely, deep down he was good. All his strictness was well meant. He wanted to keep us safe, protect us. I used to love him, I think. Did I? I used to watch for his return. I remember him telling me about the Romans draining the land; I remember him swinging me round with his big hands until I was dizzy and setting me down to totter about, but that was when I was a tiny child, when it wasn't so difficult to fathom, life didn't seem so complex. And this, after all, was his home. He would live here and it would be normal again. We'd go to church on Sundays again. I saw that Agatha's face was flushing with pleasure as the same realization grew in her. The twins looked blankly at him. The notion of any change was terrifying to them.

Father prodded about in his pipe for a moment. 'And as for your clothes,' he continued. 'Of course you must have some more. You're growing children. But I think the same style will do very well for the time being. After all, there's no one to see you here, is there? And there's plenty of time in which to grow up, believe me.'

'But I am grown up!' exploded Agatha. 'Sorry, Father,' she said quickly. Inwardly I cursed Agatha. I thought she was going to make Father mad, but he glanced at her genially.

'You've a long way to go yet,' he said. 'There's no call for you to be preening and thinking of your appearance. Vanity is a sin. I cannot encourage it in you or I would not consider myself to be doing my job as a good father. Next thing you'll be wanting to put your hair up!' he said. 'Now. I'm going to take a look in the barn, make sure everything's as it should be out there.'

When he had left the room, Agatha and I exchanged glances. This morning we each wore our hair in a long plait down our backs – Agatha's fat and smooth, my own thin and spiky – but I'd taken to pinning mine up when I saw Isaac. Of course, it didn't stay up for long for he delighted in pulling the pins out and letting it fall over my naked shoulders. Oh Isaac! And Agatha spent ages in front of the mirror playing with her massy hair, piling it up in a way that emphasized the slender stem of her neck, the delicate line of her chin. We just weren't children, that was the truth. Father didn't see us properly. Something got in the way of his seeing us properly. Aggie and I were young women, young women burning and bursting with the need to express ourselves.

All that day I felt fidgety and ill with fear. Father was here and there, good-natured, filling the house with his pipe-smoke, frowning over some papers; and later with the old tools from the barn which had become Agatha's tools, for she did all the handy work, he went round securing the window latches. He climbed up a ladder and fixed the gutter where it was pulling away from the eaves. All day I grew more and more anxious. I was yearning and aching for Isaac and yet terrified that he would choose today to come. I could not bear the thought of Father attacking Isaac, my Isaac, and so I willed him to keep away, all the time watching for him and wanting him.

The following day, Father went to the village to arrange for some men to come and paint the outside of the house. I breathed easier while he was away. I sat at the window silently begging Isaac to appear. I was tempted to run to the Howgegos', run to Isaac, and warn him and tell him I loved him and tell him I was sorry – but it would have taken too long. Besides, he might not have been there. I hoped he was not there, that he was working away for that would explain why he had not been near since our argument. It would also keep him safe from Father.

'Do you think he's going to live here again, all the time?' I asked Aggie. She was crouching on the ground weeding between the parsnips, her earthy fingers deft and sure.

'I don't know,' she said. She straightened up. 'It wouldn't be so bad you know, if he did. Things might be more . . . normal.'

'But why all of a sudden . . .' I began, and then we looked at each other, the same thought occurring to us both. 'You don't think . . .'

'Another wife!'

We were silent considering the possibility. 'Mother's been gone a long, long time,' I offered.

'Well it might make things more cheerful,' said Agatha. 'She might be nice. *She* might persuade Father about our clothes. She might let us go to the village . . . get some servants to do this,' she looked regretfully at her dirty hands.

'Yes! To the village!' I said.

'And even to town, to Ely.'

'Even to London!' The possibilities were endless. This new wife would be our ally against Father. She would be all in favour of me and Isaac. We could get married properly, openly, no need to run away. My mind ran on. And she would get Father to hire some help with the heavy work. It would be wonderful, all our problems solved at once.

'And she'll know what they are wearing in town,' Aggie said. 'And Father will be nicer, his temper will be better . . .'

We went on for some time. Already we loved the new wife, were grateful to her. It never occurred to us to doubt that we were right.

When Father came back from town, we looked at him with new eyes. Yes. That was why he seemed both more positive and more benign. He was in love. He wanted to get everything spruced up for the arrival of his bride. I suppressed any little niggles of loyalty to Mother I might have felt, for surely she would want the best for us?

'The painters are coming in two days,' Father said. 'And I'll be staying until the job's complete. I'm not leaving you alone with such ruffians. Now, after tea tonight, I've got something to tell you, some more important news.'

Agatha and I darted smiles at each other. We knew!

'I wonder what they'll be like,' said Aggie as soon as he'd gone.

'Who?'

'The painters of course! If only Father wasn't going to be here. I'd like to do my hair properly, and oh these stupid dresses!' she put her hands on her waist and pinched the material of her voluminous pinafore in. 'If only I could have a waist! Oh I wonder if they'll be handsome. Perhaps there will be one each.'

'But I don't need one. I've got Isaac.'

'Isaac!'

'Yes, Isaac.'

'You're not really serious about him, Milly. I know he's been your friend, but he's not . . . I mean you could do a lot better.'

'I don't want to do better,' I said. 'I love him.' I felt very cross with Agatha, hurt on Isaac's behalf now. How stupid I'd been ever to consider the two of them together, to mind Isaac thinking her beautiful. As far as she was concerned Isaac was beneath her consideration. Poor Isaac. 'Anyway,' I said, 'I don't know what makes you think you're so special.' I wondered what she'd say if she knew what Isaac and I did together when we were alone. I wondered if she really knew about it. I only knew because Isaac had told me.

'You've got a lot to learn, Agatha,' I said turning away from her, 'about the world and so on.' Agatha snorted, but I know I left her wondering what on earth I meant.

All through tea Agatha and I kept exchanging glances, smiles. We knew what Father was going to tell us. It was a strange mealtime. Some of the tension was gone. Father had been home for two days and there had not been a sign of his dangerous angry side. He could be so charming. It made me wonder whether it hadn't all been in my imagination. He had seemed a brute with Mother to me. But then what had Mother been? I remembered, I tried to remember, the sweetness and the songs and the fun – but there was the other side of her too. The side that could sit for hours with bleak empty eyes while we minded Ellenanesther, minded ourselves. Isaac said she was mad. Oh it is so hard to know. But Father could be cruel. Mother was never cruel. Father was charming – and cruel. I remembered the way he had been with Mrs Howgego, the way he had turned her away from the house with tears in her eyes and a basket full of goodness for us after Mother had gone. Now that I knew more of life; now that I'd seen and touched and had a man of my very own, I felt less afraid of him. Although he was a man, he seemed less immense, less of an enigma. I thought I knew all there was to know. Oh what stupidity! What arrogance!

'What do you like to do?' Father asked one of the twins, suddenly. They looked startled, Father so rarely seemed to notice them.

'We play with dolls. We clean the house. We collect the eggs,' they said in unison.

'Good,' said Father. 'Now I'm going to speak to you,' he

pointed to one of them. 'I'm sorry, child, but I have to admit that I'm not entirely certain which one you are. Are you Esther?'

'Ellenanesther,' she mumbled.

'Speak up child!'

'Ellenanesther,' they both said, very distinctly.

'Yes, I know your names,' said Father, an edge in his voice. 'Do you think I don't know my own children's names for Heaven's sake! What I want to know is which is which.'

The twins had gone very pale. 'That's Ellen and that's Esther,' I said quickly. The truth was that nobody could remember. One was left-handed and one was right-handed: that was the only difference between them. There had simply never been any need to refer to them separately. They were, to all intents and purposes, one person; a four-legged, two-headed person; a person called Ellenanesther.

'All right then, Ellen,' continued Father, 'look at me when I'm speaking to you. I want you to tell me your exact age, in years and months.'

'Nine years and ten months,' I said.

'I'm not addressing you,' said Father icily.

'Nine,' mumbled Ellenanesther, then in a louder voice, 'We are nine years and ten months, Father.'

'Can you never speak alone?' Father exclaimed. 'Good gracious! are you all right in the head? – heads,' he added.

'That's just how they are, Father,' I said. 'They've always been like that.' Father frowned at me and then at them.

'They don't do any harm,' I wheedled.

'It's like coming home to an asylum,' he said, subsiding a little.

'You said you had something to tell us, some good news,' said Agatha timidly.

Father twitched his eyes away from Ellenanesther who visibly sagged with relief. My own hands which had been knotted painfully together under the table, I allowed to relax. He began in a leisurely way to fill his pipe. 'I don't know about "good" news,' he said, 'but yes I do have something to tell you.'

Once his pipe was filled to his satisfaction he leant back and began to speak. 'As you are well aware – although I know it has had little impact on you as such, our country is at war with Germany. Since it has dragged on so much longer than antici-pated, more and more men, men with families, now are being called upon to join the army. Although I didn't volunteer in the first instance, because of my responsibilities, I now feel it is my duty to answer the call.' Aggie and I darted confused looks across the table.

'So you're going to war?' I said. 'That's what you wanted to tell us.'

'Yes,' he said.

'So you're not getting married?' Agatha kicked me under the table.

'What an extraordinary idea! Whatever made you think . . . ? Well never mind that now. Yes, I am going to France and you are not to worry. No harm will come to me, I'm certain – but even if it did, as I have explained to you, everything would be all right. I have arranged my finances so that you would be provided for, for as long as you live, as long as you remain here, in this house.'

'But if we wanted to marry?' I blurted out. I could not help it.

He paused, as if considering a surprising idea. But I was a young woman. What ever else did he expect me to be thinking of?

'You seem to have a head full of marriage this evening,' he said. 'First me and then yourselves.'

'But we *will* want to get married one day,' I said.

'That is, I suppose, a possibility sometime in the future,' he conceded. 'But there is no sense in worrying your head about such an eventuality now. We mustn't be so wicked and so selfish as to be thinking only of ourselves at a time like this.' He talked on and on until we were yawning. The war was nothing much to me. There was talk of food being rationed, but no danger that we would starve. I had pondered over news in Father's paper about unimaginable numbers of young men being killed. Isaac's big brothers were away somewhere over the sea, in France or

Belgium. I wished them well but all I cared about was that Isaac didn't go and join them. He must not. Father could go and then we would have more freedom. I needn't be afraid of his return, not for months and months. Yes, Father could go and welcome. But not Isaac.

*   *   *

It is raining harder now. The house is creaking. Agatha is moving about. Rain is dripping even into my room so it must be wet up there. Ellenanesther are mumbling still, a low buzzing like wasps. I wish it would grow light.

Whatever can be the matter with George tonight? He's never been as noisy as this, not for years. I cannot bear to think how many years he has been down there. He or she. I decided upon 'he' because George was more like a boy than a girl as a baby. When he was born, we could not tell. I said it was a boy to please Agatha, but his private place was strange, not like a boy's and not like a girl's. It didn't matter. He was no trouble as a baby. He scarcely ever cried, just a high whimper now and again to remind us he was there. It was easy to forget. He wasn't appealing, not like Ellenanesther when they were babies. When they were past the skinned rabbit stage they were lovely, rosy and fat. But George didn't have lovely skin and big bright eyes. He was all dull and yellowish with a big tongue, a tongue too big for his mouth, lolling and protruding. He was not lovable, but he was no trouble. We fed him with milk and changed him, and apart from that he just lay in the old crib that we had all slept in as babies. He just lay there for hours. Sleeping sometimes, some-times just staring out. He was like that for years.

I said to Aggie that it wasn't natural. He didn't crawl or sit up or babble, not till he was huge. He just opened his mouth for the mushy food we made him. Sometimes his tongue got in the way, so that although he seemed hungry, the food would spill every-where. Sometimes he did smile. He did learn to smile, and he still does. He smiles a toothless old man/woman's smile when I go down into the cellar to feed him.

Anybody might think it was cruel keeping him down there – but there is no alternative. When he got to seven or eight he grew more troublesome. He began to hurt himself, bang his head against the wall, bite his arms until they bled. And then he began to bite us too, or lunge at us, throw his arm at us as if it was a heavy branch. And he began to get fat. By the time he was about twelve, he was very fat. His body was even more confusing then, because his chest grew rounded as if he had breasts and his face blew up into a great pale blubbery moon.

We had to put him down in the cellar for our own safety. He was violent. He was ugly and stupid. He stank because he soiled and wet himself. We could not stand him. We could not stand seeing him or smelling him or hearing him. Agatha, particularly, could not bear to look at this monster of her own making.

He seemed interested when we took him down at first. It's a good cellar, not too damp, and it is just above the ground at the top so that a narrow slit of daylight can be seen. We put a chair down there and a bit of carpet and a toilet bucket, and straw and blankets for his bed. I can't forget the look in his eyes. As if he was interested. This was something new! An adventure. No. He was excited. No. No he was not capable of feeling that. It was just the light, a trick of the light. He cannot have feelings like that, he is just a lump, an ignorant freak. He's a monster created out of evil. He has no feelings. He deserves no pity. I will not feel guilt.

But there was a screaming when we left him there and shut the door. I would have left a candle, I would, but it would have been dangerous, and anyway there was a little light, in the daytime, from the slit of a window. He screamed and roared. He banged and groaned. He hardly let up for days. We did not dare go down until he was weak and quiet, until he had given up. When we did we found everything toppled and broken and fouled. He had not even tried to use the bucket and the stench was sickening. He had banged and rubbed his head against the wall so that the hair came out. There were tufts of his dull stringy hair everywhere and patches of his scalp were bald and scabbed. There were teeth marks and wounds and blood all over his forearms, as if he had tried to eat his arms.

Agatha came straight up out of the cellar and was sick. Strange that Aggie, so good with animals, so practical with everyday things, is so squeamish with George. But then he is a reminder to her. He is her flesh and blood. He is *her* guilt. Horrible. I sorted the mess out that time, and I washed George and fed him, and then, for his own good, I tied him to the chair. I think it was better like that. He was safer.

He was quieter too. There was an awful sobbing, a soft moaning that you could hear at night. I used to sleep night after night with my head under the pillow, but after a time he settled down.

After a time there was no need to tie him to the chair. He sat there anyway. He's not a human really, he's a freak, a heavy, ugly, stinking, drooling freak. And tonight he's a crying freak. It's a dreadful sound; a man/woman voice. It sounds frightened. But what can he be frightened of now? What is he capable of being frightened of? He's been there most of his life. What could have upset him so, now? When it's light, I will go down and see him, but I cannot now, not in the dark of the night, because yes, I am afraid. Not of the dark, but of George.

When I hear his crying and Ellenanesther's murmuring and Agatha crashing about, I think Father was right. He was seeing into the future when he called this house an asylum. I'm the only sane person here – and I sometimes wonder how much longer that can last.

We *had* to do it. We could not live with George – he was simply not livable with. We could not have had him taken away as he should have been. There are places for people like him – but how could we explain his existence? Nobody knew then, or knows now, about him. Agatha was afraid she'd be taken away, be put into prison. I was afraid questions would be asked about Father; afraid that they'd take Ellenanesther away. They wouldn't have been able to stand that, and nor would I. I would have been alone if they'd taken everyone away from me. I would have been free, but by then I had lost any desire for freedom. We thought he would die down there. I thought human beings needed sunlight. I thought he would not last many months, but he did not die. He has been a torment to us down there all these years, that man/woman, that freak. And he has lived as long as us.

*   *   *

The painters were all that Agatha could have dreamed. Two young men, strong and handsome, one of them as dark as the other was fair. Father was careful not to let them out of his sight, but he could not stop Agatha noticing the strength of their arms as they moved their ladders; he could not stop her noticing the deftness of their brush-strokes. He could not stop her hearing the light-heartedness of them: jokes and laughter!

I tried not to notice, tried to keep my mind on Isaac. Soon, soon, soon, Father would go. Go for ages, months perhaps, and then Isaac and I would have plenty of time to make our plans, to leave. It would be hard to leave Agatha and Ellenanesther. They would have to do more. I knew I would have to teach Ellenanesther to do more before I left. But then there would be the time, if Father was going away there would be plenty of time. And then it would be hard for Agatha with no one to talk to, for Ellenanesther were no company. But I knew that I must live my own life, I must. Isaac and I together, forever. There was one worry on my mind. The months were passing and something was wrong. It hadn't worked. In the months since Isaac and I had become lovers I'd been waiting for the bleeding to stop as a sign that there was to be a child. For then it would all be so simple. Mrs Howgego would insist upon our marriage then. Even Father, if we managed to get away, get married before he found out, would have no choice but to accept it. And then, once the baby was born, he'd soften, surely, once he saw his grandchild. And if it was a boy! It would take the place of the son he'd wanted, that Mother hadn't given him. Perhaps he'd give us his blessing then, if there was a son. Perhaps he'd give us his money too.

I tried sternly to keep my mind on Isaac as the painters worked. Neither was as tall as Isaac, neither as sweet. But I did enjoy hearing them joke. It was so rare to catch the sound of laughter here. They kept trying to catch my eye, or Agatha's. I sensed that sometimes when they talked, their eyes squinting up at the windows, it was of us they talked, of the girls inside the walls. It would have been so good just to talk to them, and no harm in that, surely? Just for the novelty of new faces, new voices. That would have been good. But Father had forbidden it, and he was always close by. He sat in his chair outside, smoking his pipe, working, writing letters, and occasionally criticizing one of the painters for a shoddy corner, or paint splashed on the brickwork.

Inside the house, I kept finding myself straying to the room where one of them was painting the outside window frame. I could not prevent my eyes from resting on the strong arms of the fair one. They were brown arms, covered in hairs that shone in the sun like wires. The wrists were broad, the fingers long and thick and well shaped. My awful mind kept straying to wonder if the gold of the hair on his forearms was the same all over his body; whether his legs were as strong and brown as his arms; even about the secret part of him – would that be sturdy too, thick and brown and well-shaped too? I made myself blush with such thoughts and had to leave the room where the strong arm of the painter moved back and forward, where the brush, wet and heavy with paint, caressed the wood of the frame. I left the room and went round the back to the orchard, and forced my mind back to Isaac, and his smooth freckled youthfulness, his soft baby manness.

'I am in love,' Agatha whispered to me in the cool of the evening when Father had gone early to bed.

I pulled a face. 'Which one?'

'The dark-haired one of course,' replied Agatha. 'He's by far the most handsome, the finest.'

I was surprised at the little surge of relief I felt. 'I don't agree,' I said. 'The other seems far more . . . pleasant to me.'

'Well there you are then! I said there'd be one each,' said

Agatha triumphantly. 'He's got such a wonderful nose. Noble I'd call it. And such dark hair. I could never look at a fair man.'

'What are you going to do then?' I said. 'Ask him to marry you?'

'Oh do be quiet,' snapped Agatha, and then her eyes became dreamy. 'He smiled at me today you know, when Father wasn't looking. Such a smile! It was as if he was speaking to me with his eyes.'

'And what was he saying, with his eyes?'

'Oh Milly,' sighed Aggie. 'You'll never understand.'

'I do!' I said. 'I understand more than you think. More than you. Me and Isaac . . .'

'Isaac! You and Isaac! You're just children.'

'Little do you know,' I said. I hated Aggie when she was like that, so haughty, so know-it-all.

Agatha looked at me closely. 'What do you mean by that?' she asked.

'Oh nothing,' I said. But I could not keep it in. I could not resist making Agatha feel small. 'Just that I know it all. The meaning of love.'

'The *meaning* of love? What are you talking about?'

'You wait, Agatha, you'll find out one day.'

'I don't believe you,' said Agatha, flushing. 'I don't believe you know what you're talking about.'

'Do you know how babies are made?'

'Of course I do! They're made when people get married.'

'Or when they're not nice.'

'Yes,' agreed Agatha doubtfully.

'And what does that mean? Not nice?'

'I don't want to talk about this. What if Father . . .'

I lowered my voice, for Father was indeed only the thickness of the ceiling away. 'It's what the bull does to the cow,' I said. 'Their things grow big as . . .'

'Milly!'

'And they push it inside you just like the bull and . . .'

'I don't want to hear!' Agatha whispered fiercely, blocking up her ears. 'You are disgusting, Milly. That's what comes of spending so much time with Isaac. It isn't like that. Love is more than that.' She looked at me down her nose as if I was a smudge on the wall, turned away and began climbing the stairs.

'Yes,' I called after her softly. 'Yes, it's more than that. But it is that too.'

After she'd gone, I stood alone in the kitchen for ages. I went to the window and pressed my face against the cool glass. Outside the sky was chaotic as a crumpled bed, black and grey tumbles of cloud, slits of moonlight. I whispered Isaac's name. I willed the time away until we could be together. And then I went to bed, my feet cold, the smell of the fresh paint in my hair.

*   *   *

I can hear Aggie's feet on the stairs, coming down the attic stairs. She is not asleep, I can tell by the jerky way she's walking. That is good, that she is awake.

She hesitates on the landing. Is she going down? George is making such a racket. Surely Aggie will not want to hear any more of that than she has to.

She's coming to my door. I will be quiet. What could she want at this time of night, in the middle of the night? She is tapping on my door. I do not know what to do. We do not do this, bother each other at night. The time between bedtime and dawn is our own time, private time. It is my only space. And now she comes knocking at my door! Not content to crash about above me, she has to come downstairs to plague me now.

'Milly, please,' she calls, her voice coarse as a crow's, her fingers scratching at my door like claws. 'Please, Milly, let me come in.'

We wait in silence for a moment to see what I will do.

'Open the door then,' I say. I am helpless. It is not like Agatha to plead.

She pushes open my door. 'The rain is getting in,' she says. She is shivering. 'Something must have happened to the roof. I nearly

104

got off to sleep but I was woken by the rain. My bed is wet. Everything is wet.'

'You can have a blanket,' I say. She wraps it around herself, an old parcel of bones.

'It's even getting in down here,' I say. 'Can you hear it dripping?' We are quiet, listening to the steady ominous dripping. I can hear Agatha's knees creaking. And there are the other noises too.

'What are we to do?' asks Agatha. She sounds as if she is near to tears. What *is* the matter with her? I will not be able to bear it if she goes all weak and soft. I need her to push against. I need her not to give way before me. Just because she is older does not give her the right. 'I can't sleep,' she says. 'I can't get to sleep in all that wet. I might just as well be outside and be done with it.'

'There is downstairs.'

'No,' she says, and her voice is weak and wavery. Despite myself I am feeling sorry for Agatha. Old bitch. Old witch. I must harden myself, remember her meanness; the way she's never forgiven me for having this room. Is that what this is all about? I wouldn't put it past her to damage the roof herself just to gain a claim on this room. But I am not sharing it with her. It is mine. It is all that is mine.

'There's always the cellar,' I say. She gives a startled whimper. Frightened, I realize that she is actually starting to cry. 'As if we aren't wet enough already without you starting up,' I say. She is really crying now, a hard snivelling. 'Oh, I didn't mean it.' I force out the words. I'm almost shouting now. It is so hard to force these damn words out of my throat. They stick like fishbones. They will only come if I shout. 'I'm sorry, Agatha.' Once out they hang in the darkness between us, these words, this apology like a curiosity, something to be wondered at.

'Why don't you get into bed with me,' I say, for I cannot think of anything else. I am surprised when she does that, climbs beside me into the bed that was Mother and Father's bed. There is nothing of Agatha. She's like the folding chair that Father had, the one he used to sit outside in and smoke his pipe. She's like a rickety folding chair, all sticks and creaking joints, folded to almost nothing. She is cold too and smells like a wet animal. I squeeze myself against the wall. I will share my bed with her just for tonight, but I do not want to touch her.

'Thank you,' she says. These words from Agatha are almost as rare as my own apology. But I do not want this. I have hated and needed and needed and hated Agatha for . . . ever since . . . oh I cannot be doing with this. I cannot be doing with this change. It is almost like affection.

'Ellenanesther are busy tonight,' I say, and Agatha grunts. Her breath is still shuddery from her shivers and from her tears. I do not mention the noise that is loudest, the frightful sound of George, howling now like a nightmare. Never before has he made such a din! Not since he first went down. Never.

'I've been thinking about the painters,' I say, to keep our minds off it.

'Oh, the painters,' says Agatha. 'That was a time!'

'It was only a short time,' I remind her. 'Only two days.'

'Two and a half. They came back the next day to clear up.'

'Two and a bit,' I concede. 'They only stayed an hour or two that day. Strange that they bothered really. You'd think they'd have cleared up once they'd finished, the night before.'

'Not strange really, dear,' says Agatha. Over her tears now, and warmer, her old bitch of a voice strains to sound mysterious. 'Not strange at all if there was some other reason.'

I do not answer although I know what she means. She thinks the dark one was in love with her. Poor pathetic Agatha making over her memories to suit her dreams.

'Oh he was a one!' she cackles.

'I preferred the fair one,' I say, 'though even he was nothing compared with Isaac. He spoke to me, you know, the fair one did, when Father wasn't there.'

'When was Father not there?' she demands. We've had this out so many times.

'He went to the privy,' I say, 'and while he was gone, the fair one spoke to me.'

'What did he say then? Go on, tell me what he said.'

'I really can't remember exactly,' I say as if I couldn't care less. It is true that I cannot quite remember although I have tried. Oh yes. 'It was something like, "What do you call yourself?" and when I said "Milly," he repeated it, "Milly," slowly as if tasting it in his mouth and then he paused and said, "That's a pretty name, a sweet name. That suits you, a pretty girl like you." '

'Liar!' spits Agatha. But it's not a lie. 'Anyway,' she continues, 'the dark one spoke to me. He said more to me than that.'

'What then?' I challenge.

'*I* remember every word,' she says. She settles herself down and her cold shinbone brushes mine. I withdraw my leg sharply.

'You're squashing me,' I say.

She moves away a bit, but it is difficult, the bed slopes so steeply to the middle. 'It was the second day. It was about three o'clock. Father was there, but he'd nodded off in his chair.' I consider the possibility of this. It *was* hot weather, so perhaps . . . I let it go. 'He was painting the frame of this window, Father's window. I just happened to be in here for some reason. Perhaps I was dusting . . .' Preposterous! Dusting wasn't her job! Just like Agatha to do that, pretend she had some business to be in here, pretend she didn't know he was there. 'Of course I had my blue dress on,' she says. *Of course.* 'And I walked towards the window. I didn't see him at first. I was quite unaware that he was there. I stopped in front of the mirror and I lifted my hair up, just to see how I looked, and in the mirror I saw myself and I saw him too, I saw that he was watching me.' Even in the dark, even so many years after I blush at Agatha's obviousness. If it was true. Which, of course, it isn't. 'I felt very foolish,' she continues, 'and I suppose I might have flushed a little, which always looks well with a dark complexion. The window was open. "Beautiful," he said, just breathed it so quietly I could scarcely hear. "I wish I could come inside and speak to you," he said. "I've been watching you. You are the most beautiful girl I have ever seen." I put my finger to my lips, so,' in the dark she performs, 'but he pointed down at Father and smiled. I walked toward the window and looked down and saw that Father was asleep in his chair. His papers had slipped to the ground. And then,' she pauses dramatically, 'he put *his* fingers to *his* lips, the first two fingers, the index and the middle, and he kissed them. He pressed his lips against them for a full moment like so . . . and then he reached round the open edge of the window and he grasped my hand, *my* hand with the fingers that he had touched against his lips!' she sighs with pleasure and nestles her disgusting old greasy wet head into my pillow. 'Yes, that was a time,' she says.

Of course it is all lies. What an imagination she has! Why can't she keep them to herself, her lies? She interferes with my memories when she talks such codswallop. She throws something in, something new in like that, after all this time and it sets it all askew. The past. I close my eyes tightly and squeeze out her nonsense. I will pretend to be asleep. Perhaps she will believe that I am asleep, that I did not hear that story. And then she will feel foolish.

*   *   *

When the painters had cleared up and gone, Father began to make preparations for his own departure. There was an unusual air of gaiety. It was September of, I think, 1916 or 1917. The house felt clean and smart with its new coat of glossy paint. The smell of the paint hung in the air, pervaded every corner. What a wonderful, exciting smell!

I was so excited I could barely keep the foolish grin from my face, could barely suppress a song. Agatha too was unnaturally cheerful, fussing round Father, showing just how useful she could be. Every September I think of that time. It was a warm morning, warm as summer, but with a definite edge of autumn. The angle of the sun was different. It had risen later through a pale grey mist, discovering a spangle of diamond cobwebs in the grass, the rich gleam of ripening apples on the trees.

I could not wait for Father to go. I knew exactly what I would do the minute he was safely gone. Exactly. I would set off for the Howgegos'. If Isaac wasn't there I would demand to know where he was. I needed to see him. I needed to exorcize the fair painter with his strong brown wrists and his golden hairs from my mind. Oh how I longed to see Isaac. The time was right. We were free! We could either go now, straight away, or else we could wait. There was no rush. I could invite Isaac to tea and make a cake just like his mother's, better than his mother's, and I would get Aggie and Ellenanesther used to the idea of our marriage. I could hardly believe that we had come to the end of all that furtiveness, all our fear. We need no longer live with one ear cocked for the sound of Father's arrival. When Mrs Howgego called we would be free to relax in her company, no longer afraid of the risk we were all taking.

At last Father was ready. We sat down to lunch with him before he departed. We ate plates of cold hard-boiled eggs, cold potatoes and sliced tomatoes. It all tasted of paint and pipe-smoke, but we ate with relish. When we had finished we sat waiting for a sign from Father that the meal was over, that we might get up and speed him on his way.

'We'll just have some tea, I think,' he said at last, getting his pipe from his pocket. 'I'd enjoy a last cup before I go. And then there are just a few extra details to discuss.' He filled his pipe with maddening care while Aggie brewed the tea, and I began to feel anxious. What details? A wasp, a sleepy late wasp crawled across the table. What details? Father reached over and squashed the wasp with the back of a spoon upon the tablecloth. Ellenanesther gave a little cry.

'Surely you don't want to be stung?' said Father. They looked down. 'Wasps are horrible dangerous things. No use to anyone. They deserve to die if you ask me.'

Aggie poured out the tea and Father lit his pipe and sat back with a contented sigh.

'I want to be able to think of things carrying on, while I'm away, just as they have all along. I want you big girls to mind the little ones. There will be no need for you to go anywhere. Your groceries will be delivered every fortnight by Mrs Gotobed. You can write a list when she comes. Payment is all taken care of, of course. There will be no need for you to worry about money and so on. Indeed, while you're all here you need never worry your heads about money at all.'

We scarcely knew what money was. If he knew how I longed to handle it! What a luxury, what a treat it would be to simply walk into a shop and choose something and pay for it myself.

'As you are well aware,' he continued, 'I do not wish you to have any contact with that Howgego woman or her . . .' he paused, searching for a suitable word, 'tribe. So stay away. She knows and you know, so stay away. Can I trust you?' He looked each of us in the eyes in turn.

Aggie nodded, innocent as anything, but I could not prevent myself flushing. 'Mmm,' he said. 'Just as well that I'm not leaving it all to trust. No doubt you wouldn't *dream*,' he looked hard at me, 'of disobeying my orders, of going against the express wishes of your father . . .' My cheeks were burning now. 'But, just in case, I want to keep you from temptation, from the badness that there is in the world. The sordid world. You've all got your mother's blood in your veins and I'm not risking . . .' he paused. Aggie and I exchanged glances. 'I've only got your interests at heart,' he continued. 'I've asked Mr Whitton to keep an eye. He'll help with the livestock of course, and he'll keep an eye out too. He's a trustworthy chap but all the same there is no need to notice him. I'm paying him a pretty penny, I'll tell you, to look out for you. It's an expensive business keeping a houseful of girls but never let it be said that I shirked my responsibilities.'

He looked hard at me. A new anxiety began swelling in my chest. 'All right, Milly?' he said. 'Have I said something to disturb you? Surely you'll feel safer having an eye kept on you?'

'Yes, Father,' I mumbled.

'And I'll tell you now, just to save you the trouble of finding out for yourself, that the third Howgego lad, the lanky one, the one I fancy used to be some sort of playmate of yours . . .'

'Yes?' I said coldly.

'I've made arrangements for him to be conscripted into my regiment.'

'What?' My mind was closing down. Father's face bloated with triumph.

'He's to join the army with me, my dear. I don't know how he's avoided it for so long. Some sort of cowardly conchie no doubt he took a fancy to be, but oh no . . .'

'He's not a coward,' I said. 'He had to stay at home to support his mam and his brothers.'

'You seem to know an awful lot about the domestic arrangements of complete strangers. Peasants,' he said. 'And just listen to yourself! "Mam" indeed!' He continued to open and close his mouth and sounds continued to stream out with the blue of the smoke. I held on to the edge of the table, squashing my thumbs until they were white. I watched his smug mouth talking and talking and puffing on his pipe and sipping his tea. I watched the brown beads of tea wobble on his moustaches as he talked. Oh so clever. Yes. He'd got the better of me. No wonder he seemed so pleased with himself. He'd tied up all the ends all right. I felt as if I'd been kicked in the belly. It was difficult for me to breathe. I looked down at the squashed mess of wasp on the tablecloth and then I looked back at him. He smiled at me and I smiled back, wishing him dead, wishing him a slow, agonizing death.

I went to the Howgegos' house after Father had gone. It was all true. Mrs Howgego hugged me when I cried, but her eyes were cold. She blamed me. 'I don't see as how we can stay here now,' she said. 'We were struggling with what Isaac brought in, but now . . .' She opened her arms in despair. The house was cold. There was no smell of baking or soapsuds. Bobby and Davey looked pale and pinched. They all looked poor. 'There's a cottage in the village we can have for half this rent,' she said. 'And I'll be able to work every day. Laundry and that.'

'So you're leaving?'

'We are.'

I said goodbye and I walked away. That was that. That was the best things in my life done away with. I walked the long way home, past Mother's Dyke. I stood on the top and looked into the water. Tea-coloured today, it flowed smoothly, innocently, between its muddy banks. Father had driven Mother to this. It was crystal clear to me now. He was the one. I swayed on the edge considering how it would feel if I followed her, if I simply let myself fall into the water, not jump, just fall. After all I am my mother's daughter. Her blood runs in my veins. I thought how my dress and my jacket would become heavy and soaked and would pull me under; how cold it would be; how it would fill my ears, my nose, my throat, my lungs. Then nothing would matter any more. It would all rinse away in the brown of the water.

But no. I am not Mother, and Father was not having that power over me. I would go home and I would get on with it. Life. I would wait. Isaac would be back, of course he would. It simply meant a wait. Simply *more* patience. It simply meant putting off my plans for . . . for how long? A few months? That was nothing after all these years.

*   *   *

She is sleeping now, her breath rasping drily in her throat, her mouth open. It feels strange to be so close to her. It is irritating and disturbing when we touch. I am actually afraid that her leg will rest against me. Perhaps it is just that I have lost the habit of touching? I've had so little of it really. There was Mother, of course, but I was only ten when she left me. I can't remember Father touching me apart from the odd pat on the head. There was Roger – or Roderick? – and there was Isaac. He was the only one to touch me completely. Aggie's toenails are long and yellow and horny and scaly and hooked. I pray that they will not scratch against my leg. I could not bear that.

Was it Roger – or was it Roderick – or was it true at all?

Oh the rain is streaming down. There are no longer separate drops, it just falls in sheets, folds and folds of sheets just falling, falling, as if the sky is caving in. The moonlight has been drenched. All light is gone now. There is a treble drip from my ceiling: plipplipplop, plipplipplop, plipplipplop. And there is Aggie's breathing. And there are the other sounds. If only I could sleep, just for half an hour, just for a minute or two – but how can I? I have to lie so stiff and tense to prevent myself rolling towards Agatha. Witch. It's like being in bed with a broomstick, a creaking broomstick. What if the roof gave way altogether? What then?

*   *   *

I lived in a kind of a bubble after that, a bubble within the bubble of our own curious separate existence. Now that Mrs Howgego no longer called, we hardly saw a soul. Mr Whitton was there. Watching. But he rarely spoke to us. Had Father paid him not to, I wonder? I hated him anyway, him and his bull. I got used to him, to him watching, appearing at random intervals, his arms hanging by his sides. Just watching. Just keeping an eye.

I waved at first. Tried to start a conversation, but he only grunted in reply, edged away if I approached him, kept his eyes averted. I didn't care. I hated him anyway, him and his cruel laugh. It's just that he would have been someone else to talk to. A hook to fish me out of myself. We all got used to it. It was no different in the end, having him there, lurking, than being constrained by our own fear of Father's return. It was easier really. He took over the job of our consciences. And anyway, there was nothing for him to see or know. No more Isaac. No more Mrs Howgego.

The groceries were delivered regularly. Less of this or that sometimes because of the war. I hardly noticed. I hardly cared. We didn't bother much with food, nothing elaborate anyway. Rituals that we'd carried on since Mother's death began to peel away in this odd time, this pause. We stopped eating at particular times. If no one was hungry, no one cooked. If anyone bothered to cook then everyone would eat. Ellenanesther made meals occasionally; strangely neat meals – turnips and carrots and potatoes cut into exact cubes (you'd find the odd-shaped edges rejected in the bin); meat squared off on the plate. Nothing ever touched anything else. They were not like plates of real food, although they were, of course, and if Ellenanesther cooked, we ate. And it was not only a pause.

Some days we ate only bread and butter and drank milk, standing up, separately. Sometimes we let the stove go out, although it was a devil to light. Mother had tried never to let it go out. It had been a warm heart, a centre. But now . . . A cold layer of grey ash settled and no one bothered to clean it up.

I don't know how long that time lasted. I was very far away. I spent a lot of my time just wandering about. I often walked to Mother's Dyke and thought about my mother and her despair. If only she hadn't done it. It wasn't right, it couldn't be right to leave your children like that, to leave your big girls to care for your baby girls in such a place; to leave them all in the care of the man who had driven you to this. Oh Mother. Why didn't you take us too? Or surely we could have escaped together from this gaping trap of a place? Scuttled together away from the hugeness of this sky?

Sometimes I walked past the Howgegos' old house. Once, I went right up to it and peered through the dusty windows. There was the stone sink, the staircase that curved steeply from the kitchen to Mrs Howgego's room; the worn flagged kitchen floor. It was so familiar and so different. Cold, empty, impersonal. And it was my fault, all this. It was my fault that Mrs Howgego had lost another one of her sons, and her home. I sat on the hollowed doorstep and looked at the walnut tree that the boys used to play under. There was a ragged strip of rope still dangling from the lowest branch. The wind stirred the branches and the rope swayed. The old tree moaned sadly.

Isaac would not come back. I knew that, suddenly, sitting there on the step of his home, the step that his footfall had helped to

114

wear away. There was a feeling of such emptiness there, of such suffocating sadness that I got up quickly. I must leave, I knew, before I believed in it, in the sadness. There was an old broken cart sticking out of the long tangled grass. Isaac had played on that when he was a boy. He had even cajoled me onto it. 'Scared?' and I'd said, 'No,' of course, and sat upon it, my heart thudding, my eyes squeezed tight, and he'd pushed and I'd hurtled along and hit the gate and fallen off and grazed my knee. I hadn't cried, and Isaac had looked admiringly at me as he scolded, 'You're daft you are, you should have steered.'

* * *

Quiet. Ah . . . just a moment of – almost – peace. Just for a moment everything, everyone, pauses. If only that peace would last I would sleep, I would just sink into it, let it soak into me. That is what I need, but there is no peace here, in the middle of nowhere. And then it starts again, the terrible frightening, frightened, frightful noise.

* * *

Sometimes our father sent us letters, close, clipped and cold, delivered with the groceries. In a postscript to one of these he informed us of Isaac's death. He had been shot dead, a long time ago.

Shot? Shot where? In the head? Did the bullet smash his darling fragile skull? In the chest? In that heart I'd felt the beating of against my own breast? In his soft, smooth belly? His long pale back? Shot? Shot dead.

* * *

Oh that dreadful wailing! I cannot stand much more of this! And although the rain seems to be stopping, although I think there is the first early glimmer of light in the sky, there is still the dripping. It is enough to drive you mad. And I cannot move. I cannot even breathe with Agatha so close.

* * *

And then there were months. A year? years? Existence. A sort of sleep without rest. A long dull stretch to struggle through. I suppose I ate and drank and walked and talked, but I wasn't there. Not really. I could not let myself be there, properly, not switch on my mind, properly, or I would have had to scream. For Isaac was dead. And this was no pause. This was it.

*   *   *

It sounds as if Ellenanesther are going downstairs. Yes, I can hear them on the stairs. I wonder if the rain has got into their rooms too? Tomorrow I will go with Aggie up to the attic and see how far the rain has damaged her room. We will have to make some sort of arrangement for her. I cannot endure another night with her in my bed.

*   *   *

I could not cry in all that time because I knew that if I started I would not be able to stop. There was a flood inside me, dammed inside with ice. I was dry. But the bitterness of those useless unshed tears soured my soul, aged me, made my head heavy and my face a mask of sadness. In the mirror I was a stranger. I did not speak, not for ages. My tongue grew dry and heavy. I stayed away from Agatha, because Agatha had arms that might encircle me, and if someone had held me then I would have caved in.

Ellenanesther drew more into themselves too at this time. They stopped playing games. They worked hard, in unison, and they kept things neat. They cleaned up the ash. They managed, mostly, to keep the stove on.

I kept away from Agatha, but Agatha kept going. She used to sing to herself and not just to herself. I saw her with the rows and rows of audience before her. I saw how she sparkled and flirted her dark eyes and how her voice grew warm and husky with all those strangers' eyes upon her. She should have been on the stage. She could and should, but instead she battled on. She fed the cow, she milked, she churned butter, she collected eggs, she fed the hens, she dug and planted. She sang to herself. She talked to herself too, for there was no one else. I would not talk. Ellenanesther did not bother to talk, even to each other they

116

hardly talked, there was no need. They had not the need of words, they just knew.

Aggie sang to herself but something kept happening to the words. Each time she sang the words sounded different, the meaning slipping and sliding. Words became vague. It was only the tunes that Agatha remembered now. And sometimes it was as if Mother was back, with that voice those tunes just there, just resting in the air somewhere near Agatha's industrious self.

And then one day I woke up and saw that it was spring. I really woke up. I lay in my bed and watched the way the sun filtered through my curtains and fell, a dusty ribbon on my bed. I lay still for a long time, wide awake for the first time. I climbed out of bed and looked out of the window. The apple trees were in blossom, sweet fragile pink petals against the tender green of the new leaves. In the long grass underneath, hens were pecking, and kittens stalking. A tiny tabby creature leapt at the trunk of my tree, the tree Isaac and I used to climb. It dangled for a moment, its minute curved pins of claws catching in the bark, and then it fell, a soft weight, into the springy grass.

And Isaac was dead. There was of course, only one thing I could possibly do, and that was leave. Why didn't I do it before? Oh *why* didn't I?

I dressed quickly, aware of the curious lightness of my limbs. I felt as if I was recovering from a long illness, light and ravenous. I was thinner and my hair was a long and greasy mess. I knew I must eat and I must wash and then I must prepare to leave. Mr Whitton could do what he liked, tell Father what he liked. By the time he knew anything I would be gone. I would find my way to London, find people who knew Mother's family. Father would never find me. I would be free.

Agatha was amazed to see me that morning. I prepared breakfast and laid the table properly in a way it hadn't been done for I don't know how long. I put bread and butter on the table, and a pot of honey. I put fresh milk in a china jug and I brewed tea. I picked a spray of flimsy yellow dog roses and put them in a vase on the table.

'Come on, Aggie,' I called, for I could hear her in the barn. 'Come on, Ellenanesther, breakfast.'

'Well, Milly! Well thank goodness,' said Aggie coming in quickly. 'It's nice to see you looking better.' She tried to touch my arm but I pulled away.

'I'll pour you some tea,' I said. I was shocked to see how pale she looked. There were shadows under her eyes, and sad lines. I had not really seen her for such a long time.

'Are you well?' I asked. 'You look pale.'

'I'm all right,' she said. 'I'm just glad that you're . . . back to your old self?' she looked at me quizzically.

'Yes,' I said. But that was a lie. I was not back to my old self. That self had shrivelled and died. That old self had had only one purpose – to marry Isaac. That purpose had gone: that self had gone. But it was all right. There was something left. I looked at them all anew. I looked at them with the knowledge that I would soon be gone, and might never see them again. Ellenanesther looked different. Strangely, they looked younger. There was less expression on their blank and pleasant identical faces. Perhaps I would see them again, perhaps once in London I could send for them. We could all live in London in a nice little house. We could be normal.

'But how?' said Aggie when I told her I planned to leave. 'You've got no money. You don't know how they *do* things.'

'I'll walk to the village,' I said. 'I'll go and find Mrs Howgego. I'll find a way to get to London. I'll walk if I have to. Perhaps there's something I could sell . . .' I looked wildly around. 'I'll send someone from the village to get my things.'

Agatha reached out to me again, but I flinched away. 'Don't go,' she said softly.

'I've got to go. I can't live here. I simply can't now. Not now that Isaac . . .'

'But I need you to stay,' she said, 'and Ellenanesther need you too. And what do you think will happen to you? In all that wickedness?' Agatha believed Father. She was so simple in some ways. Not stupid but gullible. She simply believed whatever she was told.

'That's just what Father tells us to keep us here,' I said. 'I don't believe it's true. Mother loved London. She wanted to go back there, and that's what I want.'

'I don't think you can,' she said. 'I don't think you'll know how to do it, live among people, find your way. What will you eat?'

'Oh do be quiet!' I snapped. I did not want to hear her voicing my own doubts. 'If the world's so wicked and terrible and impossible why does Father live in it? He could stay here.'

'It's probably different for men,' she said. She followed me around as I dragged Mother's old trunk up from the cellar. It was heavy and exhausting work bumping it up the steep steps. She did not help. It was dirty. It was mildewed. In the bottom were the faded remains of a dress. It had been a fine dress by the look of it, long and full, a dark green stuff. I pulled it out and tried to unfold it but it gave way in my hands. It fell in a flutter of dusty shreds and moths, and the smell of mildew filled the room.

'I've got to go,' I said firmly. I went up to my little room and sorted my belongings into three piles: things I didn't need; things I'd pack in the trunk and send for later when I was established; and things I'd carry with me. I took the second pile downstairs and put them in the bottom of the trunk. They looked pathetic and small, lost in there. Hardly enough to run a life on. I added some books, and then I stopped. I was at a loss. Ellenanesther stood in the doorway watching, their eyes round and solemn. Kittens were racing round batting bits of Mother's fine dress with their paws. Agatha was watching me, the bitch look on her face.

'Now what?' she said. I felt like punching her. She was watching and waiting for me to stop, to admit that this was ridiculous, that of course I couldn't go. How could I? I didn't know the first thing.

I do not know what I would have done next, whether I would

really have gone, how it would have ended, if a boy with a telegram hadn't arrived that morning. My heart leapt with joy and apprehension when he arrived with the envelope. Was he dead then? Was Father dead?

No. He was only wounded. He was on his way home. The telegram was old. He could arrive home at any time. So, of course, I could not go. I would have got to the village at least. I *would* have got that far. Even that would have been better than nothing, would have been freedom of a sort.

And how did Agatha know just what to do? How did she know to say, 'No reply, thank you,' and smile at the boy who was an ugly boy, nothing like Isaac, a sallow boy, and close the door crisply behind him before reacting to the telegram at all.

'Wounded!' she kept exclaiming, pacing around the room. 'Oh poor Father . . . but there's no indication of how! Of what sort of injury.' She was excited. Important. Oh yes, she loved a drama, Aggie did. A nurse now she was, I could see it in her face. Angel of mercy. Oh how I could see through Agatha then, how I despised her.

*   *   *

It is certainly getting light. A greyness is seeping in, showing the edges, the folds, the corners of things. The cats will start scratching soon to be let in. They will bring their furred and feathered plunder into the kitchen, gifts for Agatha. A summer dawn. I do not wish to see another summer.

Agatha is still sleeping, flat on her back in the middle of the bed so I have to squash to the edge to avoid her. Her sharp gristly nose, a crow's beak, rises out of a face that has sagged back in sleep to reveal the bones beneath the shadowy skin. She is puffing, her cheeks ballooning out, thin grey balloons, and then the air escaping through her lips in a gush. Soon I will kick her awake, kick her out. And then perhaps I will sleep.

I can see a new shape on the ceiling. It is like a map. It is a dark wet patch of plaster. Water is still dripping through, but more slowly now. It's typical of Agatha to let the leak in *her* bedroom ceiling damage *mine*. She could have put something there, a basin or something to catch the drips. The crack in the ceiling runs through the map like a wide river, a river with many tributaries cutting through a foreign land. A foreign land. France. Isaac went to France. They go all over now, Mark was telling me, Spain, America, Africa. They fly in aeroplanes. Quite often aeroplanes fly across here, loud and low sometimes, enough to give you a fright. There was another war, and there were planes too, and bombs, but that was nothing to do with us. We had no men to lose. Even in the night they fly over, waking me sometimes. In the dark the sound is ominous, but on a bright blue day, when a far-off plane leaves a trail like a scratch on the surface of the sky, I must say, I feel tempted to try. Whatever must it feel like to plunge up into the sky like a bird? But such a heavy bird. No, I don't think I could trust it. Aggie is afraid that one will fall out of the sky one day, and land on us, squash us flat. I don't think that is very likely. But if it did, it would be neat, it would be sudden, it would be final. It would be better than this gradual wearing away.

*　　*　　*

Father was wounded, yes, but not in any way that we'd expected. He'd got shrapnel in his leg and had an ugly wound that needed dressing. But that was not really the trouble. Something had happened to his head and he was not the same. He would sit quiet for hours, not hearing or not listening to us. But then suddenly he would come to and then we never knew what to expect. He might be quiet and lucid. He might be angry. He might even laugh.

Ellenanesther would not go near him, but Aggie – to begin with – was in her element. She bustled about quiet and grave and important. Her step became smooth and confident, filled with purpose. And she knew what she was doing. I cannot understand how. I certainly did not. She dressed his wound which made me sick even to think of. She took him his food, the best of food, prepared carefully herself. She spent hours sitting with him, talking about what I cannot think. She even persuaded him once or twice to play cards. I used to stay out of the way. I did not want anything to do with him. As far as I was concerned, he had killed my mother and he had killed my lover. I would have left him to rot. I resented Agatha too for her capability, for the pleasure she was getting from serving Father.

But then it all changed. He began to call her Phyllida. He began to call her whore. She changed. She grew pale and nervous, her confidence all gone. I would hear her whimpering sometimes at night. And then one day, accidentally through the crack where the door had swung ajar, I saw what he was doing to her, what she was letting him do to her. Ugly old man with his rotting leg. Fucking her. That was his word. I heard that word from him. Fucking her, not making love. He was doing it like an animal. I saw his face, red and mad, the veins in his neck bulging. I saw her face closed as if in sleep, closed, composed. But did I catch just the hint of a smile, a look of satisfaction? She had got him.

No. No. *No*. I am wrong. Agatha was frightened. I know she was. I heard her whimpering in the dark of the night. She was frightened and devoted and confused. It was unspeakable and wicked what her father was doing to her. If he was her father. I did not know, do not know. What Isaac told me sowed a seed in my mind, but I do not *know*. I don't know any more what is truth and what is lies. I don't know any better than Agatha does.

*   *   *

The light is spilling in now. I can see the coarse grimy graininess of Agatha's face. Her eyes are moving, sliding behind her thin lids. Of what does she dream? She has no lashes left, just a red rim where they have fallen out. She used to have such lashes! There is a crashing downstairs now, and the howling. Louder. What are Ellenanesther doing down there? It could *not* be nearer. My ears are playing tricks now like my memory.

And what does it matter now, whether he was her father or not? It was wicked either way. When I saw what they were doing, I resolved, again, to go. Oh I do try not to remember that time. I try to keep it locked away but in the night it will, sometimes, creep up on me. But it is not the night now. It is morning now, almost. The light. Do not think of that time. In the light, do not think. I have not thought of it for years and years but now it is forcing its way out. No, do not think. It is Agatha's fault. She is too close. Bitch. I cannot bear her so close. I cannot control my memory.

*　　*　　*

And one day I heard a screaming. Father was recovering by then, recovering the use of his leg anyway, and he was outside. I looked out of the window. He was dragging Agatha towards the barn and she was screaming. 'No better than an animal,' he was shouting at her and I could see the beads of mad spittle flying from his mouth. 'No better than your whore of a mother.' And Agatha was screaming in terror and I could not go to her. What could I have done? It had happened before. I lay on my bed. Useless, I lay on my bed. When it is over, I thought, I will be nicer to Aggie. I will help her with Father. Why is she screaming so? I could hear a curious noise, a curious buzzing mumbling noise, like a nest of wasps.

*　　*　　*

Oh that is it. That is what it reminds me of, the noise that Ellenanesther have been making tonight.

*　　*　　*

It was Ellenanesther. It could not be called speech. It was like a buzzing chant. There was a rhythm but it was not a song. It grew higher and further away and it travelled outside. Something happened to me then. I could scarcely have slept, not at midday, not with all that racket going on – but the next thing I knew I was waking up.

It was all quiet. I got up and went downstairs. There was blood on the kitchen floor; on the blue-and-white tiles; on the table; in the sink. I turned round and Ellenanesther were there. They were holding hands. They had sweet smiles on their bloody faces. 'All better now,' they said.

I found Agatha in the barn. Her dress was torn, her hair was a

123

tangle of straw, but she was not hurt. Not in any way that you could see. She was sitting in a corner, her hands clasped round her knees. Her eyes were huge dark circles in the whiteness of her face. She was staring at what was left of Father.

They had killed him with sharp knives. They had stabbed him many times. They had cut off his fingers and his thing, and lined them up beside him, neatly.

* * *

Agatha is moaning in her sleep now, struggling, her eyes sliding and twitching wildly behind her lids. I shake her.

'Wake up,' I say. 'It's all right. It's only a dream.'

She opens her eyes and stares up at the ceiling. For a moment I am not sure whether she is really awake, whether she has heard me, but then she speaks.

'It is not all right. It is not only a dream.'

I consider this. 'Listen,' I say. 'Now that it is light we will have to think about what has been happening downstairs. We will have to do something.'

She is quiet for a moment. 'It has stopped raining. That is something.'

'Come downstairs with me,' I say.

She sighs. 'Not yet. I don't want to see.'

'See what?'

'I don't want to.'

'What?' But I know. She does not want any more horrors stored up in her brain to flicker against her sleeping eyes. I know all about that, but I am not a coward, and what has to be done simply has to be done.

'I'll go first,' I say, 'but you must follow.'

The truth is that although I am *not* a coward, I am as frightened as Agatha of what we will find.

'Not yet,' says Agatha. 'Let's wait till it's properly light.'

I relent. Now that it is nearly time to go down towards the noise my heart is beating painfully. I close my eyes. I am tired after all and I should try to sleep a little. It is blood I am afraid of.

*   *   *

I pulled Agatha up off the floor. 'Look away,' I commanded. Agatha switched her eyes away from Father. There was no light in her eyes, they were huge and blank. She looked into my eyes.

'Ellenanesther . . .' she began, a hysterical quiver in her voice, 'like machines. You should have seen . . .'

'Do not think,' I said. 'Go into the house, Agatha.'

'But Ellenanesther . . .'

'They won't hurt you. Don't you see? Go into the house.'

For once Agatha obeyed me. There was a strength in my voice, a purpose that I had never heard before, and Agatha obeyed. Once she had gone, stumbling like a blind woman, I set to work. Just for once I knew just what to do. I piled straw over the body, and wood. I led the cow outside and tethered her in the orchard. She was calm as ever, oblivious. The horror had not touched her.

I chased the pecking chickens out of the barn, then I went into the kitchen. Ellenanesther were in the sitting-room, kneeling by the hearth. For the first time in ages they were playing with the old peg dolls. They were snapping the legs and throwing them into the fireplace. 'Omotheromothero,' they were mumbling, 'and a sonandaboy andaholygoat. We toll them dead. Foreveranever.'

'Stop it!' I shouted. They turned and looked at me aghast. After all that had happened, it was me shouting like that that frightened them.

'Go into the kitchen and clean yourselves up. Clean up all that blood and change your clothes.' They got up off their knees then, Ellenanesther did, like good children, and did what they were told.

I went upstairs and made Agatha take off her dress and her underwear. 'Just get into bed and stay there,' I said. 'Try to sleep. Try not to think. I'll make some tea later. I'll heat water for a bath.'

I filled the stove with wood, filled the great pans we used only for baths and washdays and put them on to heat. All the time I did this I felt strong and eager. I knew just what to do. This was work, real work, real important work, and I was the only one to do it. I lit a candle and, shielding the pale flame with my hand, carried it across the yard and into the barn.

I paused for a moment, the warmth of the flame flapping against my hand, and I looked at the place where Isaac and I had made love that first time, that disappointing time, and many times more. Sunshine slanted through the gaps in the roof lighting the floating dust particles so that they gleamed like gold. It's a lovely day, I thought, surprised. Without looking too closely at the pile of blood-soaked straw I put the candle down beside it, and piled fresh straw around it. Once it was blazing I built it up into a proper fire with wood from the pile. Soon joyful hot clean flames leapt and crackled greedily, and began to creep into the pile that had been Father. It was harder to burn this, for it was dense and wet, but I persevered. I fetched Aggie's torn dress, and the stained clothes of Ellenanesther and piled them on to add to the blaze. I piled wood and straw on top and poked and poked with a broom handle into the dense mass of it to let air penetrate. At last there was a smell that told me that he was burning; a terrible delicious smell of roasting flesh. I held my breath. The air filled with blacker stickier smoke. The fire popped and spluttered and splattered as it devoured Father. I ran backwards and forwards to the door for gulps of clean air and then back to the blaze whenever it began to flag to pile on more fuel, and to stir it around.

The smoke floated up and clung to the rafters, some of it escaping through the hole in the roof. But it was all right, the barn wasn't going to catch. This is what I feared most, for that would have created a beacon, a light that would surely have attracted attention. It would have been seen for miles and miles on every side. It was all right. But it took many hours to reduce Father to ash and bone. By the time the job was finished it was starting to get dark. I swept up the remnants, the bones and the ashes, the buttons and the pipe-stem, and dug them into the garden. Then when it was completely finished I went to the privy and I was sick.

That night we all bathed in gallons of clean hot water. We scrubbed our bodies pink and clean with coal-tar soap. We scrubbed away the stench of our father from our skin and hair, and then cleanly and calmly, we sat down and ate bread and butter and eggs and drank tea and ate ginger cake. Aggie was very quiet, but she did smile now and again, a trembly smile. It was worse for her, I suppose, because her feelings were most complicated. All her life she had adored Father. What she felt about the twisted stranger who had returned from the war, I don't know. She never said. But whatever else there was there was relief. She never asked me exactly what I'd done, though she must have seen the blackened circle on the floor of the barn.

Ellenanesther looked angelic with their sweet young faces shining clean, their long light hair spread out drying like silken shawls upon their shoulders, their toes pink and bare beneath their nightdresses.

We talked as if nothing had ever happened, as if we had never been other than normal.

'We haven't been away from here for weeks.'

'Months.'

'Tomorrow let's go for a walk.'

'If it's fine.'

'We could walk to the dyke, or the other way. We could go to the village.'

'But Mr Whitton . . .'

'But Father's back from the war now, remember.'

'We are free.'

We pondered this. 'To do what?' Aggie asked at last.

'To do anything we like! That's what it means.'

'But what do we want to do?'

'Go,' I said.

'But go where?'

'We don't want to go,' said Ellenanesther.

'Well that's all right,' I said, 'you don't have to. The point of it is that we can go if we do want to.'

'I suppose you will . . .' began Agatha.

'Oh yes. I'm going,' I said. 'I'm going to London. I'm going to look through the papers in Father's room and see what I can find. Money. Addresses of Mother's family.'

'I *would* like to see Mrs Howgego,' said Agatha.

'Well you can! We all can! We can go to the village. Tomorrow we can go to the village.'

We walked to the village. It was a long walk, a warm windy day. It all looked much smaller than I remembered, all the little houses low in the sunshine. I had so looked forward to this, dreamt of it many many times, but now I felt as if I was looking down a tunnel at the long street of houses – and they looked hardly real houses at all. Even the church looked diminished. It seemed unreal, like a flat cardboard front with nothing behind it. There was nobody about. Odd. It was quiet, flat and quiet with only the wind moving, swaying bushes, swinging a gate. We walked through the dusty village like live figures in a dream. We found the cottage the Howgegos had stayed in, but they were no longer there. An old woman who lived nearby saw us knocking and peering through the windows and she came out to speak to us.

'They've gone,' she said, 'long since.'

'Do you know where they're staying?' I asked.

'Cambridge way I believe,' she said. 'After her lad died she seemed to lose heart.'

'Which one?'

'That little fellow.'

'Davey?'

'That's the one. Croup. He had it dreadful. You could hear him from here.'

I had a little flash of memory: fat legs; round blue eyes the exact colour of Isaac's; a dribbly grin.

'Yes that's the one. Nice little lad,' continued the old woman, 'and she never could seem to pull herself together after that. Lost two of her big boys in the war . . . and then that little lad . . . that was too much for the poor soul, she . . .'

'Thank you,' said Agatha. She pulled me away. We walked in silence all the long hot way home. The dust blew into my mouth. It blew right in me and through me. I was nothing but dust walking along, dust suspended for a short time. My tongue was dust and my eyes. I saw nothing.

* * *

'I'm staying put,' said Agatha when we were home. 'Did you see the way they laughed at us?' I had no idea what she was talking about. 'People, from behind their curtains. Those women outside the church. Those boys on their bicycles. I saw them laughing.'

'I saw no one. And why should they laugh?'

'Well just look at us in our childish dresses! Look at us!'

I looked at Agatha. 'No one was laughing,' I said. 'No one even saw us.'

'That's all you know,' said Agatha. 'I feel completely . . . humiliated.' She had not cried when Father had dragged her into the barn, or when Ellenanesther had put a stop to Father; but she cried now, because she imagined people were laughing at her. Oh Agatha.

* * *

She has gone to sleep again. There are beads of sweat on the grey hairs on her upper lip. It is hot, with two in the bed. It will be a hot day. For once there is no wind and the air is still and humid. When the sun comes up it will be hot.

* * *

Well *she* could stay put. Ellenanesther could stay put; but I was going. I dragged out the trunk again, and replaced the few things that I had sorted out last time. They looked no more convincing

129

cowering in one corner of the trunk than they had before. Agatha would hardly speak to me.

'I've got to go,' I said. 'Please, Aggie, don't be angry. I wish you'd come too. Wouldn't you like to go to London? We could find out what they are wearing, the ladies in London, we could buy new clothes.'

'What with?' she said. 'I might not know much, Milly, but I do know you need money.'

I knew that too, of course. I just felt that it was a problem I would get over once I was away. The important thing was to get away. I went through all the boxes of papers in Father's room. Most of them were incomprehensible to me: complicated documents; things to do with investments and insurances and so on. The provisions made for us. I could not find anything useful, no addresses. There was nothing to do with Mother except the certificate of their marriage: Charles Edwin Pharoah to Phyllida Maisie Smith. Aggie came up to find me. She sat beside me on the bed and began looking through the papers.

I lay down on Father's bed, thinking how fine it would have been to have had this room, to have had that great open sweep of view to gaze out upon instead of the cramped mossy tree branches outside the window of my little room.

'You can't go!' said Agatha, suddenly, sharply. 'He's made sure of it. Look!' She held up a piece of paper which was covered in tiny cramped writing.

'What does it say?' I asked.

'It says what he said; that we only get money to live on if we stay here, all of us. Whether he's alive or dead or missing, the money will keep on being paid for our food and so on.'

'But *I* can go.'

'No, don't you see. It says *all* of us must stay. If you go, Ellenanesther and I will get no money. We'll starve.'

'But who will know?'

'You can't leave us, Milly! You couldn't dream of being so wicked!'

Agatha was being melodramatic as usual, but still there was truth in what she said. I closed my eyes and lay back on the bed. The surge of anger I felt had no direction. He had gone, completely gone. There was just a space, a smoky space, a blackened circle, but *still* he had control. *Still* he had control of me. *Still* I was not free.

'So you will stay, Milly?' insisted Agatha. 'You must.'

I could not answer. I could not think for a moment. I had lost my bearings again and a terrible deadness spread through me. I left my trunk, half packed, and I just stayed in Father's room.

Agatha wanted it, I know she did, but she did not dare push. She moved up to the playroom where the twins had been sleeping because *she* wasn't going to stay in a tiny room if I was having Father's room. She moved in there, but one day when I was outside she went into Father's room, my room, and she stole Mother's things. She took her silver-backed hairbrush and mirror; her eau-de-Cologne; and the pots of cream she used to rub on her face. I never said a word about it. But I knew she'd done it. And she knew I knew.

* * *

Agatha has never forgiven me for taking the best room like that. She's been longing for something like this to happen, for the roof to give way, to give her an excuse to intrude. She has carried her grudge inside her all this time. She has become old and wizened, and the grudge is as much a part of her as her nose is a part of her face. But it was not a grudge she could openly bear. Oh no! She owed me too much. She owed me my freedom, my chance to live a proper life. I stayed to help her bear her shame. I was young and strong, not a beauty perhaps, but a fine young woman. I could have, would have married. I would have had children, grand-children by now. But look at me! An old woman, an old barren disappointed woman. Oh no! She could not say a word although she did flounce around, a martyred look upon her face, reeking of eau-de-Cologne. She could not complain for if she had I would have upped and left, so instead she's spent the years crashing about up there, moving the furniture, *not* to make it right, *not* to make it more comfortable or homely, but to bother me, to punish me.

*   *   *

Because later, some weeks later, I tried again. I would go. Somehow I would get money, earn money and I would send it. *I* would support them. It was a last wriggle, a last desperate attempt to flip out of the net before I was overcome with the terrible tedium of this life. The trap of what we have done.

And who knows whether I would really have succeeded? Agatha put a stop to it anyway. She came into my room one day, when I was lying on my bed and sat beside me.

'Milly,' she said. 'You know what Mrs Howgego said about keeping ourselves nice.'

'Yes.'

'She said, do you remember? She said that the time to worry was if the bleeding stopped . . .'

'Yes.'

'And that that means there's a baby on the way.'

'Yes.' So that was his final trump. Agatha was going to have a baby. I hated Agatha then. Disgraced. A disgrace . . . Not that I cared about that. What I felt most strongly was simply pure hard cold jealousy. It should have been *me*. I'd tried and tried with Isaac, for me and Isaac, for a child of our love. It should have been me!

'I think there is a baby on the way.'

'Oh.' I turned my face to the wall.

'Milly. Please, don't turn away, talk to me please.'

'It will be a bastard,' I said. 'Like you.'

'Milly!'

'It's true.'

She sat still and quiet for such a long time that I thought she must have crept out. But then she spoke again, almost eagerly.

'What do you mean?'

'Father was not your father.'

She was silent for some time more. 'How do you know?'

'Isaac knew . . . and I heard Mother once, talking to Mrs Howgego. I didn't understand then. I didn't believe Isaac.'

'But you never said! Oh thank God!'

I turned over and looked at her. 'What do you mean, thank God?'

'Don't you see? It's not so bad then. If Father isn't my father then it's not such a terrible thing. Not such a sin.'

'Still a sin though. You thought he was Father.'

'No, perhaps I knew all the time,' she lied. 'Perhaps deep down I did know. Of course I knew! I always felt I was different, special, and of course, he knew! Don't you see? What he was doing was wrong, yes, but not as wrong as I thought it was. If he *knew* I wasn't his daughter.'

'Still wrong though. He still forced you. He still hurt you.'

Agatha was miles away now. 'It will have been the man with the ice swan,' she said, 'that time when Mother went out to dinner in the emerald dress. And there was a sea of violet petals.'

'He *did* force you, didn't he, Agatha?' I asked. She looked down. 'Didn't he?' I insisted.

'Not at first,' she whispered, her eyes down, lashes of silk against her flushed cheeks. 'At first . . . I don't know . . . something came over me, washing him, caring for him so closely. When he touched me at first I was . . . I was . . . I mean I knew it was wrong but I couldn't help it, I was almost pleased. No one touched me. You would hardly speak to me. I was lonely. And when he touched me at first, it was nice. I felt proud. He was touching me like he touched Mother.'

'Aggie!'

'It was only after I'd let him just touch me a little . . . Oh I don't know . . . I was all stirred up, remembering the painter, I suppose. I *liked* it. I suppose that means I'm wicked. I don't care. It was only after that that he wanted more, wanted to do more and then I could see it had been a mistake to start. It was wrong, but he would not stop, and we were alone so much.'

'Why didn't you say anything?'

She looked at me as if I was stupid, and she was right. I'd kept as far away from the two of them as I could at that time. And anyway, I *had* known. I should have said something, done something. I had been useless.

'And when I'd let him do it . . . like the animals . . . like you told me . . . then he went horrible. He got cruel. He started to call me names, hit me, force me.' She paused. 'I understand now, some of the names he called me. Some of the reason he seemed to hate Mother so much. It was as if he was trying to hurt Mother by hurting me. I understand a bit now. If it is true. I think it must be true, don't you, Milly? It explains why he was always cold towards me, before.' She seemed almost happy. 'It will be all right, won't it Milly? We can bring the baby up. It will be fun to have a child in the house again.'

'No,' I said. 'I must go.'

'But I *need* you Milly. More than ever before. I need you to be here when the baby's born. Ellenanesther won't be any help.'

'*I* wouldn't be any help. *I* don't know what to do.'

'I can remember a little from when Mother had the twins. But I'll need your help.'

I could remember a little of that time too. I could remember Mother's cries and the rain and the wind that blew. I could remember a basin of bloody water. I hid my face in the pillows. I could almost hear the door banging shut on me, the key turning in the lock. I was shut in properly now. Father might be gone, but he had set the seed for his successor.

So I stayed. There was nothing for it but to stay. Agatha was right: I could not leave her now. I agreed to stay and help her but vowed that I would do nothing else. No cleaning. No laundry except what was necessary for the confinement. I wasn't going to be Aggie's unpaid servant. I left the trunk where it was in the middle of the room as a reminder to Aggie of what I had given up for her. It is there still, half-full of dust. Sometimes the cats jump in and out disturbing the tatters of my clothes. We have grown so used to walking round it that that is the pattern of our walking. When I said I would do no more cleaning Aggie said then nor would she. Ellenanesther, too, soon gave up. So the same dust is there, the underlayer of dust that stirs and mingles with the rest, is the same dust that settled silently that day all those years ago – can it be sixty years? – when I gave in and I agreed to stay.

It was a strange, long time waiting for Agatha's baby. We had no idea how long it would be. She swelled so slowly, so tediously – and she made such a fuss. I am sure Mother never made a fuss like that. I'm sure she just got on with it. But Agatha! Oh she made a proper performance of it. Special food she had to have, she couldn't fancy anything ordinary. What Mrs Gotobed thought when we began ordering bloaters and anchovy essence and olives, I don't know. She'd stopped talking to us by then. And she never saw more of Agatha than a face at a window.

I began to worry as the weeks and months went by, the seasons changed and nothing happened. The cow died in that time and it was Agatha's fault. She neglected the poor thing, so absorbed in herself was she. The poor beast stopped giving milk and stopped eating and started to cough – and then one day she was dead. We did not burn her. We just left her where she was and it took a very long time for her to be reduced to bone. There was a very long time when the smell in the barn was unbearable, when on all but the coldest days the hum of flies reached the house, and the carcass was a black seething mass of them. The cats lurked too and would stalk into the house sated in the morning, their whiskers clogged with blood and grease. But by the time Agatha's baby was born she was clean bone, clean bluish bone, and they left her in peace.

One evening Agatha lifted her skirt to show us the huge mound. It looked frightening, distended and scored with red marks where it was strained almost to bursting. Her navel stuck out, insolently as a tongue. Ellenanesther and I stared at it aghast, and as we watched a knobble appeared and slid across, a knee or a heel or something. It made me feel sick.

'Sometimes I worry,' said Agatha, smiling but anxious, 'that it will never be born. That I'll just get bigger and bigger and bigger.'

'Until you,'

'Burst.' said Ellenanesther.

Agatha laughed. But I looked doubtfully at the great mound wondering privately however else it would get out.

Soon after that time, early in the New Year, Agatha came in from the barn, her face pink with cold, her eyes bright. 'It's starting,' she said. 'There's been some water, and some pain.'

She went up to her room and I put the big pans of water on to heat. She put on her nightdress and got into bed. I arranged soap and a basin and scissors and a clean sheet cut into strips by the bed, just as Mrs Howgego had done. Oh how I wished Mrs Howgego was there. How I wished it was me in that bed, that it was Agatha and Mrs Howgego who knew what to do, and that Isaac waited downstairs for the first cry of his child. But it was not so. She was like a queen lying there. So important! I would never have gloried in it like her. I would have got on with it, like Mother. You'd think it was something special, something clever, the way she carried on in all those hours of waiting. I wanted to remind her that this was a sin. This was disgrace. What she was doing was as base and mindless as what the animals did; that she was about to give birth to a bastard.

For a long time it was all calm. I did not know what to expect. Perhaps the baby would just slide out of Agatha with no further ado. But then things changed. It began to really hurt her, and hurt her and hurt her over and over. And it was like that for two days. She was gradually swallowed by exhaustion and pain. She lost her queen face, she was an ordinary frightened woman struggling like a butterfly on a pin, insignificant, a tiny battered creature writhing in this little house in the middle of nowhere under the vast empty sky. I lost my resentment for a while then. I was frightened, for I really thought Agatha would die. For two days she rose and fell over rocky mounds of pain. Sweat poured from her body, blood and greenish water seeped from between her legs. And I watched. I bathed her forehead and gave her sips of water, but I could do little else but watch. If only Mrs Howgego could have been there. She would have known what to do to help.

Ellenanesther never came into the room, but they stayed close outside, their murmuring rising and falling with Aggie's moans and screams.

At last, when I thought Aggie had got to the end of her strength, she began pushing. I watched her flesh tear and her blood flow and at last I saw the sticky crumpled screwed-up rock of the head, and then the surprisingly small slithery body covered in blood and wax and green stuff. It was dark blue and I thought that after all that it would be dead. I cut the cord and tied it with cotton like Agatha had told me and I tried to hand the baby to Agatha but she had no strength left so I wrapped it in a bit of sheet and put it aside while I tried to clean Agatha up. I thought it was going to be like Mother's time, I thought there would be another one, when Agatha started straining again, but it was only the afterbirth. I cleared it all up, holding my breath for the meaty bloody stench made me heave. I tried to make Agatha comfortable. I put on a clean nightdress and I washed her face and brushed her hair. I brought her a cup of sweet tea. I had forgotten all about the baby, so eager was I to clear up the blood. I cannot stand a room full of blood. Agatha looked exactly like Mother had looked after Ellenanesther, pale and small against the pillow, a weak child.

I picked up the bundle of sheet then and shook it a bit and it stirred. It made a tiny mewing sound. So it was alive. I wiped its face. It was horrible. A funny colour, putty grey.

'Boy or girl?' murmured Agatha, her eyes closed.

I unwrapped it and had a look. 'Boy . . . I think,' I said. Though I really could not tell.

She smiled, a tiny weak lifting of the corners of her mouth, and opened her eyes just a slit. 'So Father's got his son,' she said.

* * *

I wish he had died. I wish I had not picked him up when I did. I think he would never have breathed if he had not breathed then. Nobody ever loved him. He just wasn't lovable. Ellenanesther played with him for a while. They treated him like a doll, dressed and undressed him, laid him by the hearth, carried him out into the fresh air. I did not watch too closely. If there had been an accident it would have been for the best; but they always brought him back, safe. They soon got bored with him and his lolling head. He did not respond. He was dull and had no expression. But he was no trouble as a baby. Agatha could not bear him. She could not bear anything ugly. And look at her, now! Typical of Agatha to have a child like that. If I'd had a baby it would have been a chubby, freckly, blue-eyed child. A Howgego child.

Oh how I wish he had died. How I wish he had never been. I wish I had gone away when I had the choice. But now we must go down. The noise downstairs is terrible. It is frightening, the banging and the crashing and the howling . . . a watery sloshing sound too. But worst of all is the wasp sound of Ellenanesther, it makes my teeth ache. It is a high mad murmuring. It is rhythmic but it is not a song. We must go down now and see what there is to see. It is light now and there is no more excuse. Agatha and I must go down.

We go downstairs. Me first. Trembling. My heart is struggling in my throat, my hands are wet, slippery on the banister. Agatha follows. Because she is behind me I cannot stop and that is good. They are in the kitchen. Ellenanesther are in the kitchen. As I descend the staircase I can see them. The knife drawer is shut and there is no blood. That is good. They stand by the cellar door. They are like children in their ragged nightdresses, their faces are pink, their hair hangs long over their shoulders. They smile at me. For a moment all is calm. I might call it peace, but then, suddenly, startlingly, there is a roar from the cellar, but not down in the cellar. It comes from just behind the door. There is a roar and a crash and Ellenanesther's voices rise together in a weird chant. Oh it is not a chant, it is not really words it is . . . I don't know. The words are blurred and skewed. It is the language they made when they were tiny, when they spoke only to each other. It is something like: omotheromotheromothero thebloodandthemud antheholygoes omotheromothero . . . Oh it is no good. It does not make sense. It is maddening. It maddens me. It maddens the one who roars behind the door. Mother is no more to them than a floating face in a white hat but it is in her name that they do their terrible things. O mother. And it goes on and on and George is the loudest and when he roars their voices rise in pitch and when he is quiet they fall again. He crashes against the door.

'He is trying to escape,' says Aggie from behind me.

'That is obvious,' I say.

Ellenanesther tear their eyes away from the cellar door and look appealingly at me. 'If we had,'

'Knives . . .' they say.

'No,' I say.

'No more blood,' says Agatha. 'But he cannot come out. Why does he want to come out, now?'

'Because of the,'

'Water,' say Ellenanesther.

It is only then that I register the fact that there is water sliding out from under the cellar door and spreading across the floor. I look out of the window. The land is shining. It is not dry land any more, there is a skin of water as far as I can see, only a thin skin, pierced by the grass and the plants and the fence posts. The cellar then, is flooded.

'Look!' I say to Agatha. 'There's been so much rain . . .'

'Perhaps Mother's Dyke has gone?' she suggests.

'No, it would be worse if that had happened.'

We stand for a moment in silence looking at the shining surface all around us. It is a clean and beautiful summer morning. The sky is a tender blue and the land reflects the sky, reflects the miniature puffs of cloud. Long green grasses and leaves rise out

139

of the blueness, and underneath buttercups and clover flowers sway slightly.

'It's like snow!' says Aggie. It is not in the least like snow, but I know what she means. There is the same exhilarating feeling of waking to find the world transformed, everyday things looking new and different.

And then George bellows again. This time, along with the crashing on the door there is a splitting sound, the beginning of a splintering. Ellenanesther's voices rise so that the sound is almost painful.

'Open the door!' cries Agatha.

'Oh no,' I say. I am frightened now. I do not want to see him in the light of day.

'But he will break the door down!' Agatha screams. 'Open it. I do not want the door broken down.' She goes towards it, weak old shuffling woman.

'No!' I push past Ellenanesther who are so wrapped up in the noise they are making that they hardly notice. I lean against the door. My feet are in the wet. I can feel him bashing and battering.

'Let him out!' Agatha cries, clawing at me. 'Let him out I say. He is mine!' Oh yes. He is hers now. After all this time when she's never been near him. After all this time when I, only I, have kept him alive. But she is right. The door will break if there is much more of this, and then there will be no shutting him out.

I move aside. Her twisted fingers fumble with the bolt, and then as he pushes and roars, as he batters and crashes, she slides it to and the door suddenly bursts open, pushing her aside, and he emerges in a rush of water, a wet and bloody monster. He is white and fat in the bright light like a bloated pond creature, his hair has almost gone; his head is bruised and bleeding. His long soft nails have peeled back with all the scraping at the door. He is soaking. Water runs down him as he lurches and staggers and stumbles. He has never learned to walk, not properly. He falls on his knees in the water which is at least an inch deep now. He looks at Agatha and he blinks his tiny eyes sunk in the white lard of his face. And he smiles.

Agatha screams. Her hands cover her face. She screams and pulls away from the fat tattered hand that reaches for her leg. She backs away, backs herself up the staircase.

'Make him go back!' she stutters. It is peculiarly quiet in the kitchen now that George has stopped, and Ellenanesther have stopped. George makes tiny contented grunts and there is the sound of water lapping. 'Make him go back!' Agatha insists more loudly. There is an edge of hysteria in her voice.

I cannot move. I cannot stand it. I cannot stand the way he smiled at Agatha. There was a look like gratitude on his face. As if he remembers Aggie. As if he is capable of feelings. No no *no*. Of course he's not! How could he be? Just look at him, hideous freakish thing, drooling and swaying now.

'Yes, he will have to go back,' I say. I look at Ellenanesther. I cannot bear to touch him. I would not be strong enough. He is heavy – though in the light I am surprised he is not bigger. In the gloom of the cellar he seemed almost endlessly massive but he is quite an ordinary person size, though grossly fat. Agatha has retreated to half-way up the stairs and she sits clenched there, her bony hands gripped round the bones of her knees. Ellenanesther move towards him, their faces pleasant, and they begin to make their infernal noise again. They move towards him, one each side: 'Georgeygeorgeygeorgey intotheholy thewaterywaterywatery,' and they each place a hand on the folds of lard where his arms join his body. Their fingers sink in the fat. He balances a moment. He seems to be looking straight at Agatha. At his mother.

'Oh just do it!' she screams, and hides her face in her hands. Ellenanesther push hard at his fat womanly chest. His face is blank though he seems to resist. But he doesn't understand. He doesn't know. It's not the same for him as it would be for us. He does not feel. For a moment nothing happens. Ellenanesther's voices rise with the effort and then he topples back. He over-balances back. He doesn't cry out. Doesn't cry or roar. There is just a wallowing, a horrible billowing bubbling. And then there is silence.

It is difficult to close the door because of the water. But we do, and unnecessarily bolt the door. Ellenanesther go into the sitting-room and kneel before the hearth. 'Omotheromothero,' they begin, but softly, sweetly. Agatha goes back to her wet room. I go to mine and get into bed and stretch out. Oh it is so peaceful now that that is done! It is so quiet. It should have happened years ago. I think that now I'll sleep.

When I wake it is still and quiet. Strange. I lie listening for a few moments to the silence. Something is different. Everything is different. It takes my old brain a little time to remember what has happened. There is a significance in the air. There is a wet stain on the ceiling that looks for all the world like a map of an island cut in half by a great river with many tributaries. And then I remember.

It is *so* quiet. But I can hear a watery lapping and there is a creaking. The house is complaining. Agatha moves upstairs. Did she go to sleep in all that wetness after all? As she moves across the floor a piece of plaster falls from my ceiling and breaks softly on the floor. It looks as if last night's soaking might have done it, as if the ceiling might finally fall in.

But it is such a beautiful day. The sun is hot. It is strange to wake so late. It must be nearly lunchtime. From my window I can see the pretty sparkle of water. It is not deep. You can see through it to the grass and weeds, and yet it reflects too, the few wisps of cloud, the fence posts, the brambles that clamber over the privy, the tangle of bramble and briar, honeysuckle and clematis. It is so clear that in the distance I can see the spire, the tiny finger of the church, wagging at heaven.

I am hungry. I think today that Mark will come. There will be biscuits and olives and gin. There will be instant food from China that only needs a stir!

I have not been upstairs for a long time. Can it be years? But I make my way now up the bare curved staircase to Agatha's room. I tap on the door.

'Yes?' she says, her voice a surprised croak.

'It's Milly,' I say. 'Can I come in?' After all *she* came into my room last night. Into my bed, even.

'Of course,' she says as if there could be no question, as if there is no need to ask. Oh Agatha! Never straightforward. Her tone of voice says it all, says, 'You might be peculiar about letting me into your room, but I am not so petty. I am above such things.' I don't care any more though. It is different today. I will not rise to her bait.

She was not exaggerating last night. Her room is completely soaked. What's left of the old carpet squelches under my bare feet. Her bed is dark with wetness and it is not just rain. There is the smell of pee. At least I have not come to that. The plaster has fallen off the ceiling so that you can see the tiles – and the gaps in the tiles.

'How long has it been like this?' I ask.

She shrugs. 'It's been getting worse lately.' It looks to me as if it has gone too far to mend. There is a hole in the corner of the floor too and the dressing-table leans crookedly towards it. Mother's pots of cream and her brush have fallen off. It looks as if the floorboards are rotting away. 'So you see I can't stay in here any longer,' she says.

I have to agree. I wonder whether she will be able to sleep here again. There is a little leap inside me. Of fright perhaps? No, exhilaration. The house cannot last much longer, not now the roof has gone. There is a chink of light. There is an end in sight.

In the hot green brightness of the attic with the sun shining through the green glass and the holes in the roof, I can see how shrunken Aggie is. She looks hardly alive, as if something has gone from her. My old witch, old bitch of a sister, is just a poor old woman, a poor old woman who wets the bed. At least she didn't wet *my* bed. At least *I've* never come to that.

'Last night . . .' she begins.

'Let's have none of that,' I say. 'Last night was last night. Look what a beautiful day it is! Let's go and find some breakfast.' She hesitates. 'I'll tell you what,' I encourage, 'Mark will be coming soon with the biscuits and the stuff that only needs a stir and . . .'

'The gin!' Eager now, she follows me down.

There is not much left to eat, and there is an inch of water on the kitchen floor. The cats come in, one, two, three, and the rest. Their belly fur is wet and they pick their way disdainfully through the water and leap onto the table miaowing and straining towards Agatha.

'Hello, my poor babies,' she says, scratching and stroking as they rub eagerly against her hands. 'Are my babies wet then? Come to Mother, my poor wet pussy cats.'

No. Not much left. Just as well that Mark is coming today. And then what a feast we'll have! Good hot tea with a dash of gin, and a plate of biscuits: bourbons and pink wafers, garibaldis, gipsy creams. Oh yes delicious!

I squat just outside the door. There is no point going further, no point going outside at all really, for the same water is everywhere. But still, it isn't right to do it in the house, not like Agatha. Ellenanesther are in the sitting-room. I put on the kettle. The stove is still alight, just smouldering. There is heat enough to boil, slowly, water for a cup of tea. Then one of us will have to go out and get a log from the barn. There is a horrible sound from the cellar, but only if you listen hard. It is a dull bumping, like a log in the water. Do not listen. Yes one of us must fetch some wood from the barn. Plenty of water, anyway!

Although it is a hot day, paddling in the kitchen is no great pleasure. After a while, the water begins to irritate. It makes the tops of my feet itch where it laps as I move. Things float in the water: rubbish, leaves, dead mice and eggshells and spiders, and there is a scum of hairs.

'I suppose it will go down?' I remark to Agatha.

'I suppose it must,' she says. Neither of us so much as glances at the cellar door. The kettle is beginning to moan a little and I tip the old tea-bags out of the pot. I tip them straight into the water on the floor. After all, it will all have to be cleared up.

'The floor will be clean, anyway,' I say. 'Let's have our tea before we do another thing – and there are a few cream crackers.' I put the teapot, cups, a punctured tin of condensed milk and half a packet of (soft) cream crackers on a tray, and carry it through to the sittingroom. We sit together sipping the sticky sweet tea, our feet lifted up on the chairs away from the wetness.

Aggie balances her teacup on the arm of the chair and she puts on her stage face, old chin tilted, rheumy eyes flashing in a worldly way. And then she stands. She holds out her dress and she begins to dance. She dances round and round the trunk holding out her skirt, splashing and sploshing, filling the room with her ripples. She hums as she moves and then she remembers the words and she begins to sing. And she sings and she flirts at us as if we were an audience of men.

> She sang like a nightingale, twanged the guitar,
> Danced the cachuca and smoked a cigar;
> Oh what a form, Oh what a face!
> And she did the fandango all over the place.

And then Ellenanesther stand up too. They stand up and sway to Aggie's song, and then they join in. They have never done that, not sung a proper song like that with words and a tune. And I cannot resist it. I cannot resist joining in too. And we dance around the room and the sound of the water splashing almost drowns our voices. And we make such a racket we don't hear Mark's little green van scudding through the water.

And suddenly he is there, at the door, the heavy box crammed with our food in his arms. He is wearing long green rubber boots. I open the door and cry 'Hello!' and there is something strange about my face. I can feel it stretching. I am smiling, not

just smiling but grinning. He smiles back and he looks surprised.

'It sounds as if you're having a party, ladies,' he says.

'No, no,' I say. And the stupid grin will not leave my face.

He looks uneasy. 'I've brought you your stuff and there's some
post here for Miss A. Pharoah, but Mam says I'm to say you're to
come back with me.'

'I beg your pardon?' says Agatha. She tries to scrabble the box
from his arms.

'Just a mo!' he says. He strides right into our kitchen in the
wonderful boots and puts the box on the table. 'That's a relief,' he
says. 'That's bloody heavy, 'scuse my French, with all them tins.'

Agatha has the bourbons out and opened and has retreated
to the sitting-room before the cats smother the box, purring
and rubbing their faces against the food that they know is for
them.

'You can't stay here,' says Mark, looking at the filthy water.
'That's bad enough now but there's been a warning that the big
dyke might go – and if that do . . .'

'Oh we'll be all right,' I say blithely. For of course, that is the
answer. 'Come on, pussies,' I say, pushing the beastly things off
so that I can reach the Beefeater Gin bottle, and the letter
addressed to Aggie.

'But you don't understand,' says Mark. 'There int anyone else
living this side or there'd be more of a palaver. But that's
dangerous. You need . . . what's the word? . . . evacuating.'

'Evacuating!' I smile. 'Listen to me, young man. I've lived in
this house all my life and I'm not about to start being evacuated
now.'

'But look at the state of the place,' he says. 'Even if that drain
don't give way you can't stay here. You'll catch pneumonia.'

'Agatha,' I call, 'Ellenanesther. Come in here a minute. This
young man's got some idea about evacuating us.'

They come splashing in. Agatha has chocolatey crumbs round
her mouth. She eyes the gin bottle.

'Evacuating us?' say Ellenanesther.

'That's incredible,' exclaims Mark. 'Did you see that, they said that together, exactly.'

'Oh they always do that,' I say. 'They always have.'

'But . . .' He looks at them and they stare back. He looks away, their double gaze is too much for him. 'Look you . . .' he appeals to Agatha who looks by far the most decrepit. 'You don't want to stop here do you? Look, your dress is wet up to the knees. You'll catch your death.'

Agatha pops a bit of biscuit in her mouth, and sucks it against her gums.

'And there's a warning that the dyke's packing up,' he says. 'God knows what'll happen if that does. You'll all be washed to kingdom come.'

'Kingdom come,' repeat Ellenanesther thoughtfully.

'There they go again,' says Mark. 'Look, why don't you just put a few things together and hop in the van,' he appeals. 'You can stop at Mam's house tonight and then I'll have you back first thing tomorrow if it's all clear.'

'No,' I say. It is too late for that. Escape is the last thing on my mind. 'Thank you,' I add, for there is no call to go forgetting manners now.

'No,' say Ellenanesther. He watches them speak in unison and then turn and paddle out of the kitchen, every movement doubled before his eyes. He shakes his head in wonder.

'No,' says Agatha.

'Well, all right then,' he says. 'If you're sure.' He's given in already! A bit of a weak character then, really. I can't see Isaac giving up that easily. 'What about next fortnight's order?'

'Oh just the same,' I say. I don't add, 'if we're still here,' although I think it and so does he.

'Well I'm off then,' he says. 'They can't say I didn't try. I don't want to hang around this side of the dyke any longer than I have to. Enjoy your Pot Noodles!' He wades out to his van, then turns and looks back, 'Are you sure you won't?'

'Absolutely,' I say. And his little shiny green van sweeps away, cutting a path through the water, sending ridges of waves back to us to stir the rubbish in the kitchen.

It is peaceful in the house. Oh, the fabric creaks, and plaster trickles every now and then from the ceiling. The cats purr, piled up now in the hot dusty sun on the windowsills. They have gorged themselves with sticky brown meat and now they dry out, their feet blissfully far from the wetness.

I find a dry log in the barn, on the top of the pile, just clear of the water. I stay in there for quite a time, thinking, remembering. More of the roof has gone – though it's better than the roof of the house. I stand and look at the place where Isaac and I were together. I remember the thudding of his heart. I remember the sounds he made . . . but I do not quite remember his face. I wonder if Mark has done it yet? I think he would be a tender lover. The bones of the cow are there in the corner, a fan of ribs softened and furred with cobwebs and dust. I cannot see the place where the floor got burnt that time. The water has rinsed it away.

It is a hot afternoon. The surface of the water outside is buzzing with life. Such sudden life. This water so suddenly here is already teeming with wriggling buzzing life. I think of leeches. I go inside.

And there are treats in store. That is what life is all about, should be all about. Treats. On the table are four plastic pots, like squat vases. POT NOODLE, it says on top, *Sweet and Sour Chicken flavour*. The kettle is on. My mouth is watering. I nibble olives as I read the instructions. *Peel off lid. Pour on boiling water to 'Fill Level' on container. Let stand for two minutes.* STIR WELL. *Let stand for two minutes more.* STIR AGAIN. As simple as that! This is the life! Fancy discovering, only now, that it can be as simple as this.

And then there will be another pot of tea, strong, with gin and a thick dribble of condensed milk and pink wafers to dip in. Oh yes, this is the life. You can keep your palaces and your shops and what have you. You can keep your aeroplanes.

The kettle boils. I think that I need eye-glasses for I can't see any 'Fill Level' on container. Of course it's me that's cooking. If you can call it cooking. But even Pot Noodles are too much to ask of Agatha. No more use than ornament, big sister Agatha. But never mind. I'll just fill them to where I think. One, two, three, four, there. And a good stir. There are dried peas and all manner of bits and bobs floating about in there. And the smell! I've never smelled anything like it. I'll be glad to get off my feet, out of all this wet. Perhaps . . . Yes I know. I'll invite them upstairs to my room. That'll surprise them. It's a long time since we have all eaten together. It will be like a picnic on the floor of my room. Yes. We can carry the Pot Noodles and some forks, and a tray with tea and gin and biscuits. It will be a change. It will be fun. There are some little packets here. What do they say? *Soya Sauce. Add sauce according to taste.* Parcels of sauce! Well what of it? Tea-bags were an oddity once. But you have to move with the times. I remember the first time we had tea-bags. Was it Sarah Gotobed who brought them? No, it was well after her time, must have been one of her sons or grandsons. 'Try these, ladies,' he said. 'Much more convenient.' And after he'd gone, I caught Aggie snipping the corners off and pouring the tea into the pot. She thought the tea was put in the bags to measure it out. For people with no spoons.

The Pot Noodles are delicious. They are hot and filling. A proper hot meal. It's a long time since we had a hot meal other than everlasting omelette; it's even longer since we all ate together. It feels good, as if the water has drawn us all together. And of course there is no moaning. No trip to the cellar to dread. I have such an appetite. The sun shines into my room lighting the old sagging bed – those blankets could have done with a wash – and illuminating the plaster that hangs in clots now from the ceiling.

'My poor pussies,' says Agatha. 'They don't like the water. What will they do?'

'Oh they'll be all right,' I say. And then I remember the letter and I give it to her.

'It's from the bank,' she says, holding it up and squinting. I think her eyesight must be going faster than mine, she fumbles at it so, or perhaps it's just that she's had more gin. In the end she puts it down, unopened, unread. 'I don't need to read it now.'

Agatha fidgets. She has never learned to relax. She likes to be doing. 'What shall we do?' she asks.

'What would you like to do?'

She looks at me confused. 'The knitting is all wet,' she says.

'Let's just sit,' I say.

She fiddles with the empty noodle pots. 'These are nice,' she says. 'We could use them for something.'

Ellenanesther are sleepy. They are worn out, you can see by their faces. Their eyelids droop.

'Lie down on my bed if you like,' I say. I don't want them to leave the room. None of them. I want all my sisters here with me. It feels like the centre of the house, this room. It is a large sunny room, quite dry. We can stay here now. The sun shines through the window so hotly that it is like a hearth. It is nice to have my family all around me. Ellenanesther lie on the bed. They lie facing each other, but not touching. They fall asleep almost immediately, their blue eyes closing at the same instant.

'We could use them for cups,' says Agatha. 'I might have used them for plant pots once.'

We sit in silence for a moment, then something crashes downstairs, splashes to the floor. 'The sitting-room ceiling,' I guess. 'It had to go sooner or later.'

There is an odd twang, a complaint from Mother's piano. 'It doesn't like the wet,' I remark.

Agatha laughs and when she laughs I almost like her. Her face is transformed. You can see something of the girl Agatha, and something – the merest trace – of Mother.

Aggie hums a snatch of the fandango song again. 'If Mother's Dyke does give way,' she says dreamily, 'a twelve-foot wave will sweep the countryside destroying everything in its path.'

We sit and ponder this. Really, since the house is falling down around us; since we are old and mad; since we are murderers; I cannot think of anything fitter.

*

I drain the teapot and put a big splash of gin in each of our cups. 'Remember the painters?' I say, smiling at scraggy Aggie, such an aged stick.

'I do,' she says. 'Oh I do!'

'Well I'm sure he loved you, truly. The dark one with the noble face. I'm sure he would have married you. I bet he dreams of you still.'

She closes her eyes with the pleasure of this. Ellenanesther's breath is the rustle of leaves. I do feel strange. I think it is called content.

ABOUT THE AUTHOR

Lesley Glaister was born in Wellingborough in 1956.
She teaches a Masters Degree in Writing at Sheffield
Hallam University, and writes regular book reviews for
the *Spectator* and *The Times*. She is the author of *Honour
Thy Father*, which won the Somerset Maugham and a
Betty Trask award, *Trick or Treat, Digging to Australia,
Limestone and Clay, Partial Eclipse, The Private Parts
of Women*, and most recently *Easy Peasy*.
She lives in Sheffield.